P9-DWS-119

THE CRYSTAL CITY

NANCY ETCHEMENDY was born and raised in Reno, Nevada. Many of her poems have appeared in small literary magazines. THE CRYSTAL CITY is her third novel. She lives in Menlo Park, California, with her husband and son.

THE CRYSTAL CITY

Nancy Etchemendy

SCHOLASTIC INC.
New York Toronto London Auckland Sydney

No part of this publication may be reproduced in whole or in part, or stored in a retrieval system, or transmitted in any form or by any means, electronic, mechanical, photo-copying, recording, or otherwise, without written permission of the publisher. For information regarding permission, write to Carol Mann Literary Agency, 174 Pacific St., Brooklyn, NY 11201.

ISBN 0-590-35465-5

Copyright © 1985 by Nancy Etchemendy. All rights reserved. Published by Scholastic Inc., 730 Broadway, New York, NY 10003, by arrangement with the author.

12 11 10 9 8 7 6 5 4 3 2 1   9/8 0 1 2 3 4/9

Printed in the U.S.A.   28

First Scholastic printing, April 1989

For
Angela and Tommy

With special thanks
to All Things Considered
and the Mysterious Man from Arizona.
Also to John and Nina,
without whom Osmyrrah
might never have come to pass.

Contents

OSMYRRAH

(Oz-muh-*rah*)

A mingling of pleasant
aromas

CHAPTER ONE

Copperdust and Spiders

WILLIAM AND MAGGIE MURDOCK MADE their way slowly up the side of a gigantic, purple crystal. Maggie stood on a narrow ledge panting with exertion in the thin air, while William tried a special climbing method above her. He wedged himself into the chimney-like channel between two natural crystal towers. Then, with his back pressed against one wall and his grip-sole boots against the other, he inched upward.

"Come on, Maggie. It works. It's not that hard," William called down to her.

"In a minute. The air's so thin up here. I haven't caught my breath yet."

Maggie looked up at him, a little frightened. William, two years older than she, often did things that seemed foolish and dangerous to Maggie. Nevertheless, she longed to be more like him. William was daring and heroic, she thought wistfully. And those were things she would probably never be.

Maggie sighed and rummaged in her beltpack for a trail snack—river nuts and a dried grape-apple. She would have preferred chocolate cookies, but the cocoa trees didn't seem to like the climate or the soil of the volcanic crater where the colony was located. Most of the food in the New Genesis colony came from native plants, which were easy to grow.

Popping a river nut into her mouth, she gazed at the wide plain below the crystal. The gently sloping cones of volcanoes, some extinct and some still active, dotted the barren landscape. Airborne particles from copper-dust storms made the sky green, and Earth II's huge sun bathed everything in reddish orange light. Maggie still found the colors and the sweeping vistas disconcerting after the snug, familiar surroundings of the starship where she was born.

"Boy, it's a lot different from the Genesis, isn't it?" she said between bites.

"It sure is," said William, smiling as he stopped to look down at her. "But I guess that's just as well."

Maggie nodded, silently remembering their last days aboard the starship Genesis. The squeal of air leaking from the ship's damaged hull had filled the corridors, and even Captain Stone thought they were surely doomed. Maggie still had nightmares about it sometimes. If it hadn't been for her own brother's courage and determination, they would never have reached Earth II in time. The colonists owed their lives to William and his mysterious friends, the Watchers of Space.

William's pleasant laughter broke through her daydream. "Come on, slowpoke. I'm almost at the top."

"Coming." Maggie finished the grape-apple and brushed her hands on her bright orange coveralls.

She stepped toward the narrow channel between the crystal towers. The amethyst surface was as smooth and slippery as glass. Only the tiny suction cups on the soles of their boots made it possible for the children to attempt this climb at all. Maggie fitted herself into the shiny, purple channel and began to inch toward William, who was now perched at the top of the lower tower.

Her progress was slow. Several times she began to slip and was only barely able to stop herself by jamming her back hard against the crystal.

"Don't worry, Maggie. Easy as pie," William encouraged.

She closed her eyes and struggled upward, stubbornly refusing to cry out even when she was most frightened. As she reached the top, William helped her up beside him.

Maggie wiped her forehead and sat still, catching her breath.

"What a view!" said William, squinting into the wind. "Just think. There's a whole planet, waiting to be explored. Look at all those volcanoes. Hundreds of them. And every single one has a crater, just like our Mount Jackson. Who knows what we might find."

William's enthusiasm was contagious. "Yeah. I'll bet a lot of them have rivers, just like ours," said Maggie.

"Yep. And wherever there's water, there could be life. Maybe things we've never even imagined."

For a moment, William and Maggie sat without

speaking in the peach-colored sunlight, looking out across the plain. Below them, other giant crystals glittered beneath the green sky. Now and then, wisps of steam and ash escaped from the mouth of a cinder cone far to the northwest, Smoky Top, which the colonists were in the process of exploring. Six or seven kilometers south of their crystal perch stretched a complex range of extinct volcanoes. Among them stood Mount Jackson, which contained the shallow crater where the colonists had settled after their arrival on Earth II. One of the planet's three moons rode high in the sky, a ghostly pink pearl against a backdrop of emerald silk.

Maggie pointed. "Hey, what's that?"

On the distant horizon, a huge green cloud boiled up from the ground.

"Oh-oh," said William. "That looks like a copperdust storm. I've never seen one so big. We'd better get back home fast!" Copperdust storms were so thick and came up so fast the emergency shelters the colonists always carried when they left New Genesis were useless.

William clambered back toward the crystal channel. "Come on. I'll go down first so I'll be below you if you slip," he said as the wind began to rise.

Going down proved more difficult than climbing up had been. It was much harder to keep from slipping. Moreover, the children were anxious because of the dust storm; hurrying made the crystal more treacherous than ever.

Just as Maggie stopped herself from a dangerous slide, William gave a startled, inhaled scream. Above the high moan of the wind, Maggie heard the rattle of loosened crystal fragments. She suddenly realized that her brother was falling.

"William!" she cried.

Helpless, she watched as William plummeted down the channel, slipped on the ledge at the bottom, and tumbled headlong into a heap of greenish black sand at the base of the crystal.

Abruptly, everything disappeared from Maggie's mind except the urgent need to reach William's side. She was never quite sure how she managed to scramble so quickly down the crystal without falling herself.

When she reached the pile of sand, she found William sitting up rubbing his head.

"William! Are you okay?" Maggie dropped to her knees beside him.

"Ow. My head feels awful," he groaned. His fingertips were smeared with blood where he had touched his scalp.

"Here. Let me see," said Maggie. Among his thick blond locks she found a small, oozing cut. "Well, it doesn't look too bad." She took off her neckerchief and pressed it against the wound.

"Thanks, Maggie. I'll be okay. But we'd better get moving. That storm's coming fast." William struggled to his feet. Swaying, he would have fallen if Maggie hadn't steadied him.

"I'm so dizzy," he said. "My eyes won't focus."

"You *are* hurt, aren't you! You shouldn't have tried to stand up so fast."

By now the wind had risen to a howl, and William shouted over it, "We've gotta get moving. The storm!"

Maggie nodded as she pulled goggles and a dust mask from her beltpack. She buckled them on hastily, then helped William with his own.

"Here. Lean on me," yelled Maggie. "Which way do we go?"

"I . . . I don't know. I can't see very well."

"It's the sand. Just the sand. You'll be okay." Maggie squinted through the fine greenish dust that already filled the air. With the goggles, she could still see fairly well, and she knew that if William could not, it must be because of the bump on his head. She crossed her fingers and hoped it wasn't too serious.

"I . . . I think Mount Jackson's that way," he shouted, pointing away from the crystal.

"Okay. Here we go."

With their backs to the furious wind, William and Maggie staggered off in what they hoped was the direction of Mount Jackson and the New Genesis colony. But before long, the air was opaque with copperdust. Fine particles of green sand began to sift through their masks.

"What can we do?" cried Maggie. "It's getting hard to breathe."

"I know. I know. But I've got to stop and rest," panted William. "I'm so tired and dizzy."

"Not here, William. This storm's too much for our dust masks. We can't stop. We'll die."

"I can't go much further!"

Maggie strained to see through the dust. A large, dark shape loomed not far in front of them. Maybe it was a flow of cooled lava.

"Come on, William," she shouted, dragging him toward it. "I think there's something ahead."

As they got closer, Maggie saw that her guess was right. They had found a wall of black lava, long since cooled into solid rock. They groped their way along it slowly.

"Maybe we can find a cave," said William, gasping for air.

"That's what I was thinking." Lava walls were often honeycombed with hollows formed by air pockets trapped as the rock cooled. Most of the pockets were tiny, but the children had found a few in the past that were large enough to crawl into.

Just when they thought the green dust would surely choke them, William yelled, "Hey, what's this? There's kind of a corner here."

Maggie felt the rough wall. It turned sharply. "It's a pocket!" she cried in relief. "Not very deep, but better than nothing. Come on." Quickly, she guided William inside.

The pocket offered very little shelter indeed, but as Maggie had said, it was better than nothing.

William sat shakily on the bumpy stone floor, pulled off his goggles, and emptied his dust mask. "I guess I hit my head harder than I thought."

"I'm just glad you're alive," said Maggie, shaking out her own mask. "I hope we'll be okay here for a while."

"Me too," said William. "It was stupid of me to let us get so far from home."

Maggie shook her head. "How were you supposed

to know there was going to be such a huge dust storm?''

"I should have thought of the possibility. I know they sometimes come up fast like this." William leaned back against the wall of their shallow shelter and closed his eyes. "Boy, am I dizzy."

Maggie coughed and sputtered as a puff of green dust surged through the entrance. With fumbling fingers, she replaced her goggles and her mask.

"Come on, William. Get down on your stomach. Keep your face close to the ground," she urged. "We'll just have to wait it out."

Together they lay face-down, side-by-side on the floor of their hollow. Murmuring about the pain in his head, William fell asleep almost immediately.

But Maggie stayed awake, apprehension swirling inside her as wildly as the sand swirled in the wind. Every child in New Genesis had to take a first-aid course before the age of eight. She knew it was bad for someone with a head injury to fall asleep, but no matter how hard she tried, she couldn't rouse William. Breathing deeply and evenly, he lay with his head cradled on his arm. On the back of his sunburned hand, a tiny spot of white light gleamed. Maggie touched it softly, half hoping for a miracle.

A miracle wasn't completely out of the question, she thought as she gazed at the spot. For the miniature white star on the back of William's hand was the mark of something quite incredible—his friendship with a race of magical aliens.

Maggie sometimes lay awake at night, wishing she had been there when Orion the Watcher sealed his friendship with William by giving him the star sign. She had seen Orion herself once, but only through the clear port of the ship's observation cone. She had seen him smile and beckon as he floated in space. She should have been afraid, for he was huge, many times taller than any man she'd ever seen before. He looked like something out of a fairy tale or an ancient myth—a gigantic, fierce hunter who glowed like a golden sun. Yet somehow he didn't frighten her. Even then, she had felt certain that he came in friendship. And she had been right.

It sometimes made her angry that William never told her the whole story of what happened after that. He refused to talk about it. She knew only that he disappeared for a time, without explanation. Everyone in the starship thought he was lost forever. But he returned after all, carrying with him the special fuel that saved the ship. It wasn't the fuel, though, that Maggie was thinking of now. William had also brought back a gift from Orion—a magical sword named Starnight, with which he could summon the Watchers if he ever needed help.

As she lay beside William on the rocky floor of the lava pocket, Maggie tugged at her hair and longed to have Starnight within reach. If the sword were here now, there would at least be a chance of someone's coming to their rescue. But it was no use hoping for something impossible. The magical sword lay kilometers away in their cabin at Mount Jackson. All she and William could do was try to survive the storm and make their way home alone when it was over. She hoped that luck would be with them and that William would feel better when he awoke.

* * *

Maggie sat up with a start, realizing that she had slept without meaning to. William lay still beside her, covered with fine, green dust. The wind had stopped.

"Wake up, William. The storm's over," she said, shaking him gently.

But William didn't move.

"Hey, the storm's over." She shook him a little harder. He did not respond.

Alarmed, she turned him over and pulled the goggles and the mask away from his face. The dust clung everywhere, leaving a green film except where the goggles had sealed it out. Only his steady breathing told her that he was still alive.

Maggie felt suddenly quite alone in the cold stone hollow. What could she do? She would never be able to get William home by herself, and leaving him was out of the question.

She ran her fingers through her hair, releasing a shower of green dust. The storm had confused her so completely that she didn't know where Mount Jackson was anymore. She struggled to keep from crying. The sun would be setting before long, and on Earth II, night lasted twenty-five hours. She had to get help for William, and fast.

Crouching to avoid hitting the ceiling, she made her way to the lip of the hollow. Outside, the world was silent. Volcano cones stood everywhere she looked, but none of them seemed familiar. She squinted at the horizon, hoping to discern the ever-present steam from Smoky Top, but the air was too thick and hazy. The reddish sun hung nearer to the horizon than she liked.

Maggie guessed there was no more than an hour or two of daylight left before the long night set in. She would have to find a better shelter before then and figure out a way to move William to it. Either that, or risk suffocating in the tiny lava pocket if another storm came up.

She ducked back inside. From William's beltpack she took their emergency shelter. It was made of strong, water-repellent fabric and had telescoping legs fashioned from the tough, springy reeds that grew along the Jubilation River in the Mount Jackson crater.

On an anthropology diskette about the ancient cultures of Earth, she had read about the Plains Indians of North America. They had invented a kind of sledge that could be used for transporting bulky loads—a travois, the diskette had called it. By stretching the shelter between the telescoping legs, she thought she could make a travois for pulling William along behind her.

After a couple of false starts, Maggie managed to fasten the shelter securely across the reeds, even though, in the process, she broke the penknife she always carried. Rolling William carefully onto the travois, she lifted one end and dragged it out into the open.

As she looked up, intending to survey the horizon and pick a direction, Maggie almost dropped the travois. With a little shriek, she jumped back.

Before her stood what looked like a gigantic spider. It was almost as tall as Maggie! Like most creatures native to Earth II, it had six legs. They were thick and oddly jointed, each one ending in a group of small tentacles. Light brown hair covered its body. It glared at her with three shining, black eyes and moved its huge jaws silently up and down.

Maggie stood rooted with terror, too frightened even to scream.

CHAPTER TWO

Pursuit Among Crystals

MAGGIE'S HEART THRASHED LIKE AN ANIMAL in a cage as she stared at the spider creature's terrible jaws. She had no weapon. Her penknife lay in two pieces in her beltpack; it would have been too small to do much good anyway. And she could not run without deserting William.

She shrank back as far as she could. The thing was making a series of buzzes and clicks, slowly moving its hinged mandibles. She squeezed her eyes shut, praying that the creature would not decide to pounce on her.

Something sticky and furry touched her face. Here it was, she thought, the end of everything. She and William were about to become a spider's dinner.

"Oh, William! Please wake up!" she wailed.

But just then, a strange fragrance cascaded over her. She smelled something like flowers, mixed with a more subtle scent that reminded her of the Jubilation River on a cool, windy morning. At the same time, something warm touched her eyes, gently forcing them open. The spider's furry jaws hung before her, only centimeters from her face. Maggie screamed.

Immediately, the spider jumped back, almost as if it, too, was frightened and edgy. Maggie screamed again, on purpose this time. The spider took another step backward and stood clicking and buzzing at her as it had before. It touched its body with the tentacles at the end of one leg. Then another wave of the same strange fragrance drifted across the sand.

Maggie's pattering heart slowed down a little as curiosity replaced her fear. The more she looked at the spider beast, the less ferocious it seemed. After all, if it wanted to kill the children, it could easily have done so by now. For the first time, she noticed a large bag hanging behind one of its legs. The bag appeared to be held on with a strap that ran around the creature's body. It was made of what looked like big, leathery, brown leaves and was definitely not a natural part of the spider. But there was something even more surprising about the spider. A large, flat disk glittered on the fur of its back. The disk had a design on it, fashioned from bits of colored crystal. It looked almost like a piece of jewelry.

Though the colonists had done quite a bit of exploring since their arrival on Earth II, they had not come across a single creature that showed signs of intelligence. Maggie scratched her head as she watched the spider. She found it hard to believe that any ordinary animal would carry a pack or wear a decoration on its back. Maybe she had discovered the first intelligent native on the planet. If so, perhaps the spider beast's buzzing and clicking were not just random noises. Maybe they were a form of communication. As Maggie listened to the strange sounds, the spider touched its body with its tentacles again. This action was followed as before by the scent of flowers and water.

Still buzzing and clicking, the spider stretched out one of its legs. It did this several times before Maggie realized that it might be pointing at something. Cautiously, she glanced in the direction the spider seemed to indicate.

She cried out in spite of herself, for on the horizon loomed another of the ominous green clouds. A second copperdust storm was approaching.

Maggie turned to the spider and cried, "Please let us go! Can't you see, if you keep us here any longer, the storm will catch us. We have to find a better shelter."

The creature gazed at her with its three wet obsidian eyes. It did not move. There was only one way out. She must try to get around the thing somehow.

Tucking a large, sharp stone under her arm in case she had to defend herself, Maggie gathered her courage and began to drag the travois past the creature. It made no move to stop her. Encouraged, Maggie quickened her pace as much as she could. But a second later she realized with a rush of despair that she had no idea which direction was best. All the volcano cones looked alike to her, and she couldn't even guess which ones might offer a safe shelter and which ones might offer only a long, fruitless climb. She fought to stay calm as she looked about the plain, hoping she might spy the entrance to a cave or a deep lava tube.

As she turned around, Maggie was surprised to find

that the spider beast had followed and now stood nearby pointing at the dust cloud again.

"I know! I know!" she shouted in exasperation. "But I can't tell which way to go, and I have no idea how to ask you for help."

Grimacing, she muttered, "Oh, this is silly. I know you can't understand."

Almost as if in answer, the creature emanated a complex array of smells accompanied by further buzzing and clicking. There were tart smells like fresh fruit, musty forest scents, and spicy fragrances a little like the precious cinnamon and ginger the colonists grew in greenhouses. There were smells like wind on warm rocks. And there were smells like lightning and copper-dust clouds.

Maggie stood still. She was beginning to wonder about those smells, and the ease with which the creature seemed to produce them. She felt certain there must be some message in the chain of fragrances, but there was no time to decipher it. No time for anything. The wind was rising again. She squeezed her hands into tight fists at her sides.

Suddenly, the huge spider beast scuttled past Maggie and plucked William from the travois.

"Put him down!" cried Maggie. "Leave him alone!"

She remembered the sharp stone she had picked up. Without thinking, she lifted it above her head and threw it hard. It hit the creature's carapace with a hollow *thunk* and bounced to the ground. The spider barely seemed to notice. Buzzing loudly, it hoisted

William onto its back and skittered away across the plain.

"Stop! Stop!" screamed Maggie. But the spider paid no attention.

She started off at a run, already far behind William and the spider. Panting, her sides aching, Maggie managed to keep the creature in sight. Once, she had to drop to her hands and knees in the sand, her head drooping as she tried to catch her breath. On the plain, the planet's atmosphere was thin, and it was several minutes before she could breathe easily again. Nevertheless, when she scrambled to her feet and began to run once more, William and the spider did not seem much further away than they had before. Was lack of air affecting the way she saw things, or had the beast waited for her? She could not be certain.

The increasing wind tore at Maggie's clothes and filled her hair with sand. Still, she kept going in dogged determination. Green copperdust swirled through the air as the first fringes of the storm cloud reached her. She put on her goggles and her dust mask and tried to run faster. It was growing more and more difficult to keep the spider in sight.

Straining to see ahead through the stinging green dust, Maggie discovered that she and the spider were climbing a gentle slope. Were they heading toward a volcano, she wondered? She found it increasingly hard to keep up. Stubbornly, she refused to think about what might happen if she lost sight of William and the creature.

Instead she concentrated on forcing her aching legs to go up and down, up and down. She was gasping again, worse than ever. The air was heavy with dust, and her mask, which needed to be thoroughly cleaned between storms, was now almost useless. A fit of coughing seized her, and when she glanced up again to check her progress, she could hardly believe what she saw. It looked as if the spider, and William along with it, had disappeared into a solid rock wall! As she stood, uncertain, in the choking dust, one possible answer occurred to her. Perhaps there was a cave in the wall ahead.

By the time she reached the rocky escarpment, the storm had caught her. The world was a dense, green cloud of copperdust, and the air rose like an opaque curtain before her eyes. As much afraid for her own life now as she was for William's, Maggie groped in confusion among the jagged volcanic formations. Suddenly, she felt something smooth and sharp—a crystal, or perhaps a vein of obsidian. Feeling her way along it, she stumbled through the mouth of a gigantic, crystalline cavern.

Maggie lay panting on the cave's floor of translucent blue-green quartz. Lifting her goggles, she gazed about in wonder. Phosphorescent minerals clung everywhere in great soap-bubble shapes, faintly illuminating the walls. Huge columns of crystal shot up through black deposits of cooled lava. Blue, green, and violet shafts glimmered in the soft light. Just outside, the storm seemed very far away, part of some other world.

Maggie clambered to her feet. Dimly, she heard the spider's familiar buzzing and clicking. A faint scent of flowers and clean water lingered on the air. She had found the right place. Spitting green dust from her mouth, she stumbled off in pursuit.

Through drifts of azure sand, over thresholds of obsidian, among glittering stalactites and stalagmites, Maggie followed the sound of the spider beast. As if humming to itself, the creature purred and clacked continually. Even in the echoing cavern, the sounds made a beacon of sorts. Maggie never got very far behind, though she wondered how much longer she could keep up the pace. She had to rest briefly several times, but always when she struggled up again the spider seemed no further ahead than it had been before.

The passageway swept on and on. Maggie wondered where they were going. She suspected that the tunnel, which curved in a series of wide, gentle arcs, was the lava tube of a volcano. The temperature in the passage felt comfortable—neither the deep cold of dead mountain caves, nor the sulfurous heat of an active volcano. Perhaps the tunnel was warmed by geothermal springs or other traces of volcanic heat from an active past.

Rounding a long curve, Maggie skidded to a stop. Several meters ahead, the passageway opened into orange sunlight. Before her in the tunnel stood the spider beast, William still motionless on its back. Shaking, Maggie picked up a chunk of crystal and inched forward.

"Please give my brother back to me!" she cried thinly, breathless from her long run. She took the crystal in both hands, trying to look as fierce and capable as possible.

The spider retreated a step. Maggie breathed a sigh

of relief as it gently lifted William down from its back and laid him on the ground. It retreated several more steps and stood without moving as Maggie rushed to William's side.

William was covered with green dust from the storm. He looked parched. Maggie ripped the water canister from her beltpack and held it to his windburned lips.

"Maggie," he croaked as he drank a little. His breath came in short, frightened gasps. "We've got to get away from that thing. Can't let it hurt us!"

Maggie held his head up so he could drink more easily. "I might be wrong," she said, keeping a wary eye on the spider beast, "but I have a feeling it's not planning to hurt us. It just led us out of the biggest dust storm I've ever seen."

"Got to get away," whispered William.

Maggie frowned. She was tired and sore. She wished William would just relax and trust her for a change. "William, I'm doing the best I can," she said. "It's not that easy. It's almost dark out, and there's a huge dust storm, and I don't know where we are. There's no way we could get back to Mount Jackson right now short of calling your friends, the Watchers. And I don't even know how we'd do *that* without Starnight."

William closed his eyes and shook his head. Maggie watched in amazement as two small tears left tracks in the green dust that powdered his cheeks. "No, not the Watchers. I can't call the Watchers. I swore I wouldn't, after . . ."

"After what? William, what's the matter?"

"Sleep," he murmured. "Just need to sleep. I'll be okay."

"Oh, William!" she moaned as he dropped off to sleep again. His fear of the spider beast gave her the jitters. It made her doubt her own intuitions. What if he were right? What if the creature were leading them into some kind of trap?

She looked at William's head. The cut was not bleeding, but there was a huge lump. She pushed her lower lip out and blew her dusty hair away from her eyes. How could she trust someone who had just knocked himself silly by falling off a rock, especially when the creature in question really *had* saved them from the storm?

Maggie squinted at the spider beast. It was pointing to something beyond the lip of the cave. Brandishing the chunk of crystal, she stood up and walked cautiously toward the dusky sunlight.

She stopped, dizzy with the spectacle that greeted her. The tunnel opened on a wide, crystal shelf partway up the rim of a volcanic crater. The crater was enormous, much larger than the one in which the colonists had made their home. Its walls soared high enough to protect it from any weather, even the copperdust storm that raged outside on the plain. Far below ran a wide, turquoise river, meandering through lush meadows and forests. On the banks of the river stood a city that looked as if it belonged in a fairy tale. Carved from living crystal, its spires and towers stretched gleaming toward the sky.

"It's your city, isn't it?" she said softly.

In answer, the creature pointed first at William, then down toward the city again.

The delicious fragrance of flowers, water, and spices enveloped Maggie as she replied, "All right. If that's what you want."

CHAPTER THREE

Osmyrrah

DESPITE HER INITIAL RESERVATIONS, MAGgie's trust of the spider beast grew as she accompanied it down the obsidian trail to the crystal city. Perhaps it was because of the tender way it seemed to look after William. Perhaps it was because the creature really had saved their lives already. After all, the spider had treated the children gently, even though Maggie had thrown stones at it. Slowly, what was left of her wariness melted into anticipation. She imagined herself and William returning to Mount Jackson, triumphant explorers with news of alien friends. Ever since their arrival on the planet, the colonists had been searching for evidence of intelligent native life. After all the searching, Maggie Murdock had discovered intelligent aliens all by herself. Maybe she really had finally done something heroic!

The trail was broad and well maintained, though a little too steep for human comfort. The creature, whose tentacled feet stuck like suction cups to the glassy path, scuttled smoothly along, bearing William with no sign of difficulty. Maggie was thankful for her grip-sole boots, without which she would surely have slipped and fallen.

Now that Maggie could keep up without strain, the spider beast was silent. She wondered whether it had made the buzzing and clicking noises specifically to help her follow it through the cavern. Though the creature made no noise, there were other sounds to be heard as they approached the floor of the crater. Hidden creatures cooed sleepily from the shelter of trees that looked like silver spears topped with starlight. The milky turquoise river gurgled as it splashed through a bed of rounded crystal and obsidian pebbles.

Spider beasts basked and buzzed in the sunlight on its banks. Some of them swam in the warm, steamy current or lay submerged in quiet pools among the rocks. Maggie stopped for a moment and watched, mouth agape, as a group of bathing spiders played what looked like a juggling game with half a dozen crystal spheres that hovered in midair. The balls appeared to move by themselves whenever a spider beast pointed its tentacles at them. Other spiders rode silently above the city, encased in transparent bubbles filled with water. Wind whispered in the tall blue grass of the fertile meadows. The breeze carried with it a faint, aromatic scent like wood chips and dust. Maggie felt as if she must be dreaming.

The children's escort led the way through a tall crystal archway and onto the main thoroughfare leading to the city. Soon a retinue of curious spiders surrounded them, jostling for a look at William and Maggie. The creatures buzzed and clicked noisily, and the air was soon filled with their complex and extraordinary smells. Maggie edged closer to William as she walked, imagining what might happen if *she* came strolling through the colonists' crater with two spider beasts at her side.

But their escort seemed unruffled, and the creatures kept their distance. Though they appeared curious and excited, only one of them tried to touch the children. The children's spider replied with a sharp buzz and the sudden smell of lightning, and the offending beast scuttled away.

They had not gone far into the city when the spider beast turned through the door of a stone-and-crystal dwelling, leaving the onlookers chittering outside. The house was beautiful but completely bare of furniture. The slanting rays of the setting sun poured through translucent walls decorated with crystal mosaics.

Soft golden sand covered the floor. The spider scooped out a little hollow and laid William down in it. Then, buzzing and clicking once more, it wheeled about and disappeared through the doorway of another room. Maggie stood motionless for a moment, bewildered by the events of the past few hours. Silently, she watched the little rainbows that shimmered on the walls and floor of the room.

She looked at William, sleeping with a frown on his face. She shook her head and smiled. "I wish you would just trust me," she said. Tired and oddly happy, she lay down beside him and drifted into dreams of wind chimes and crystals.

* * *

Maggie awoke gradually to the sound of William whistling a tune as he splashed in a warm, sandy pool. She rubbed her eyes. She felt as if she'd been asleep for years. They were still in the crystal house, or in *some* crystal house.

"About time you woke up!" William called as he ducked under the water, gurgling happily. "Osmyrrah and I thought you were going to sleep forever."

"Huh?" said Maggie. Something tickled as she propped herself up on her elbows. Looking down in astonishment, she discovered that she was wrapped in a huge puff of silver cotton. Her coveralls lay beside her, spotless and crisp as if they had just been laundered. They smelled like the breeze in the spider beasts' crater—fresh and woody.

"Hey! How did my coveralls get clean? What's going on, anyway? What's all this cottony stuff?"

"I guess they don't have towels or blankets here. Osmyrrah chopped these silver puffs off a funny-looking tree for us."

"William, stop teasing! Come on. Who the heck is Osmyrrah? And why are you so smiley, anyway? I thought you were scared to death of the spider creatures."

William ducked under the water and came up again, snorting and spitting. Steamy rivulets cascaded down his shoulders. When he opened his eyes to gaze at her, there was a dimple of puzzlement in one cheek. "You know that bump on my head? Osmyrrah healed it with some kind of mushy stuff made out of plants. I don't know exactly what was in it. I just know I feel great now." He blinked and looked down into the water. "I guess I shouldn't have been so suspicious."

"Are you sure? Let me see," said Maggie. She scrambled to the edge of the pool, spraying sand in all directions and nearly losing her cottony wrap. But though she searched through William's hair for several minutes, she could find no sign of swelling or of the shallow cut that should have been there.

William smiled at her. "See? It's as if it never happened. Osmyrrah woke me up to put the stuff on my head. Then I went back to sleep, and when I woke up again I felt as good as new." He shrugged. "At first I thought I must have slept a lot longer than it seemed— long enough for the bump to heal by itself. But I went outside and looked at the moons a little while ago. And I think only about twenty hours have passed since we got here. It's almost dawn."

Maggie sat down in the sand with a jolt. *"Only* twenty hours!" she said, wrinkling her nose. "I've never slept twenty hours in my life."

William climbed dripping from the pool and wrapped himself in his own puff of silvery cotton. "I know. Either they gave us something that made us sleep, or we were awfully tired." He sat down beside her at the edge of the pool.

Maggie gazed longingly at the little wisps of steam that rose from the surface. She was covered with copperdust and dried sweat, and her legs ached from all the walking she had done. She didn't really feel as if she'd been drugged. Maybe it wasn't so amazing that she had slept for twenty hours. She had probably needed it.

"How's the water?" she asked.

"Great," William replied. "It's as warm as a bath. I think it's a geothermal spring. It runs right through the house."

Maggie tested the pool with one toe. Satisfied, she untangled herself from the cotton and slid into the water. It felt delicious. She sat down in the middle where the water was deepest and let the wavelets lap at her chin. "Okay," she said. "So when are you going to answer the biggest question? Who is Osmyrrah?"

"You know—the spider thing. The one that saved us from the storm."

She splashed, hugging her knees. "The spider thing? How'd you find out its name?"

"I didn't really. I just made it up. But it's a good name, don't you think?"

Maggie scowled. "Oh, spacefire. I thought you'd figured out how to talk to it."

"Well, no, I haven't had *that* much luck." With his heel, William traced a figure eight in the sand. "But I'm pretty sure I've discovered one thing, at least."

"Me too," said Maggie. "I think they communicate with smells."

"Yeah," said William. "You noticed it, too! Then I'm *not* crazy. You know that smell of flowers and rain the spider sometimes makes?"

"Yeah. Strange, huh? It smells like those roses they grow in the greenhouse, doesn't it?"

"Well, I think that's the spider's name. She keeps

pointing to herself, then sending out those smells. It's funny . . .''

William slowly rubbed his hair dry. "I don't know why I even remembered it. A long time ago I was looking through one of the ship's old dictionaries. There's this word—*osmyrrah*. It means . . . let's see . . . 'a mingling of pleasant aromas.' It seemed like the perfect name for her."

"You're so crazy! How do you think of these things?" said Maggie, grinning.

William shrugged, obviously pleased with himself.

"Anyway, I'd like to know why you think it's a she," said Maggie. "For all we know, these weird spiders might have three sexes, or maybe none at all."

"I know," said William, wiggling his toes as if the greatest news of all was yet to come. "I thought of that. But then I decided it was just too hard to keep calling Osmyrrah 'it,' especially when she's so friendly." He scooped up a handful of sand and took two pebbles from it, one black and one gray. He held them up for Maggie to see. "So I got two rocks, stuck them in my pocket, and shook them around. I figured if I pulled the gray rock out first, I'd call Osmyrrah 'she.' If the black one was first, I'd call her 'he.' " William smiled and tossed the pebbles back into the sand. "The gray one came out first, so I've been calling her 'she' ever since."

"William, what a crazy idea. You must have knocked your brains loose. I never thought of that spider as anything but 'it.' Leave it to you to figure out the weirdest possible way of deciding what to call her."

Maggie shook her head and grinned at the satisfied look on William's face.

"I'm starved," said William as he stood up and put on his own freshly cleaned coveralls. "I'm beginning to think these spider beasts never eat. Anything left in our beltpacks?"

"I think so," said Maggie. She climbed out of the pool and dressed while William raided their beltpacks for the remainder of their food supply.

Hungrily, the children finished off their packets of dried grape-apples and river nuts.

"I wonder if Mom and Dad are out looking for us," said Maggie as she sipped water from her canister.

"I wouldn't be surprised," replied William. "Even though it's dark, and not a very good time to look for someone, I bet they're pretty worried by now."

"Just wait till they find out where we've been, though! This is big news, William."

"It sure is. But . . ."

Before William could finish his sentence, three spider beasts appeared in the doorway. William and Maggie recognized the smallest of the three as Osmyrrah. As the children stood wondering what would happen next, Osmyrrah pointed to the spider on her left and produced a smell that reminded them of fresh, ripe peaches. Pointing to the one on her right, she produced a fragrance not unlike that of a pine woods.

"Well, meet Peaches and Forest," Maggie whispered.

"Yeah," said William. "But I wonder who they are, and how they fit into this. I've never seen them before."

William stepped forward and pointed to himself. "William," he said slowly and distinctly.

Osmyrrah produced an unusual, two-syllable buzzing noise.

"Did you hear that? She said my name!" William grabbed Maggie's arm excitedly.

"That wasn't your name," Maggie scoffed.

"Yes it was! Listen." And pointing to himself, he repeated his name.

"William," buzzed Osmyrrah blurrily. Though the sound was distorted, there could be no mistake. The creature had said William's name.

Maggie tried the same technique.

"Maggie," said Osmyrrah.

"She said it! She said it! Do you know what this means?" cried William, fairly jumping up and down. "We'll be able to communicate! We'll be able to talk to them."

After a moment of complex clicking, the larger of Osmyrrah's two companions stepped forward, holding out the foremost of its legs.

"William, I think it wants to touch you," Maggie whispered.

"I think so, too." William stiffened, fighting the instinct to pull back from such a strange-looking creature.

The spider reached up and gently touched William's face, moving from there down one of his arms to his hand, which it examined with great curiosity. It seemed to be comparing William's fingers with its own mass of small, sticky-tipped tentacles. Throughout the process, the creature emanated a steady, oddly reassuring odor that the children could not quite identify. It was at once sweet and pungent, spicy and musty.

At last, the spider stepped back as if in satisfaction, reached into the leather-leaf bag it wore, larger than Osmyrrah's, and handed William a shiny box with a small, crystal design inlaid on the top.

"What is it?" asked Maggie.

"I don't know. Looks like it's made of some kind of wood or something."

"Open it."

"I will . . . I will. Just let me figure out how." His hands trembling, William discovered a catch on one side. When he had released it, the box swung open on concealed hinges.

"Why, there's a pile of leaves inside it!" exclaimed William, kneeling to set the box down in the sand.

"Not just leaves. Look. They're covered with marks. Hey . . . I bet it's some kind of book!" Carefully, Maggie lifted one of the leaves from the box. The leaf was jet-black and supple. Both sides of it were covered with intricate marks that looked as if they might have been applied with a brush dipped in white ink.

"Darn it!" said William, wide-eyed. "I wish we had a book diskette and a pocket reader to show them in return."

"Well . . . at least we can show them that we know how to write." Maggie smoothed out a large patch of sand. With one finger she wrote, "WILLIAM." She said the name aloud and pointed to her brother. The spiders crowded around her as she wrote, "MAGGIE," repeated it aloud, and pointed to herself.

The three beasts clicked and hummed as they contemplated the symbols scrawled in the golden sand.

"Hey, look," said William suddenly, pointing past them. The walls of the crystal house had begun to brighten with the ruddy light of the rising sun.

"Daybreak already!" said Maggie.

William began to pile the leaves back into the box. "We'd better go, Maggie. The whole colony will be out looking for us. Mom and Dad are probably worried sick."

Maggie looked at the three spider beasts and the lovely crystal walls, feeling rather sad. "I hate to go just as we were starting to make progress."

"I know. So do I. But we can't do everything at once. Don't worry. We can come back tomorrow. This city isn't going anywhere."

"I'm not so sure," said Maggie, unable to hide her disappointment. "Doesn't it seem a little strange to you that none of our exploring parties have ever found this place? Even the orbital photos didn't show any craters with cities in them."

William looked up at her. "Maggie, you know this place is not some kind of mirage. I don't know why it wasn't discovered before. But we can figure that out later. There's probably some simple explanation. In the meantime, we've got to get back to Mount Jackson before somebody gets lost looking for us."

Maggie glowered. Irritated at William's superior manner, she turned around without a word and began to shove her scattered belongings back into her belt-pack.

"Here," said William, handing the carved box back to the spider. "Thanks very much. It's beautiful. But we really have to go now. People will be worried about us."

"They can't understand you," Maggie sniffed.

William turned toward her and snapped, "Well, what am I supposed to do? Just walk away?"

Maggie felt the blood rising in her cheeks. "Why do we always have to do what *you* want to do? Why are your ideas always supposed to be better than mine? We don't have to just walk away, you know. We could stay here with the spiders until they do understand us." Her eyes began to water and she swiped angrily at them with her sleeve.

William's face softened a little. "I'm sorry, Maggie," he said. "I'm just worried because I always seem to be in trouble for breaking rules, and I'm afraid we'll be punished if we don't get back as soon as we can. I didn't mean to be so bossy."

Maggie spun away from him, pretending to adjust her beltpack. "All right," she said. "But you should have told me that in the first place."

Their three hosts accompanied the children into the street. Outside, a crowd of spiders made way for them, drawing back as if in respect.

"Our friends must be pretty important," said Maggie.

"I think they are," replied William. "I didn't get to do much looking around, but Osmyrrah seems to live in the biggest house on this street."

Maggie looked at him quizzically. "I wish we could really talk to them. I just had the strangest thought. You know, maybe Osmyrrah's just a kid—like us. Maybe Peaches and Forest are her parents. Wouldn't that be something?"

William grinned. "Sometimes I think you're as crazy as I am."

Before long they reached the point where the wide, obsidian trail disappeared into the crystal cave. There the spider creatures halted, buzzing loudly. The largest one, Forest, handed the box back to William.

"You want us to take it with us?" he asked, wrinkling his forehead.

For answer, Forest thrust the box more firmly into William's hands.

"Thank you!" said William. "Believe me, a lot of people are going to be very interested in this."

Clicking, Osmyrrah broke away from Peaches and Forest and stepped toward the cave entrance. She seemed to be telling them she would guide them back outside.

"Thanks again," said Maggie, waving. With a last look at the broad, meandering river and the spires of the crystal city gleaming in the red morning sun, the children ducked into the cave.

When they emerged, they blinked in the bright, peach-colored sunlight. Below them lay the panorama of the plain, interrupted only by the black cones of volcanoes and the glittering shafts of giant crystals.

Buzzing and clicking in her now-familiar way, Osmyrrah led them down the slope of the alien volcano and onto the floor of the plain.

"Maggie, do you have any idea where Mount Jackson is?" asked William.

"No. But I have the feeling that Osmyrrah knows exactly where it is. I think we should trust her for a while and see what happens."

William shrugged. "I guess we might as well."

By and by, William and Maggie saw that Osmyrrah was indeed leading them toward one particular volcano in a chain of mountains, the outlines of which grew steadily more familiar.

"You've done it, Osmyrrah! I knew you would. You've led us home!" cried Maggie, as she spied the ashen trail that ran down the outside of Mount Jackson. Osmyrrah touched Maggie's shoulder softly and produced a mild fragrance that reminded her of the hothouse cucumbers her father sometimes sliced into salads.

William grinned. "Look behind us. The alien crater is hidden in that cluster of volcanoes. I'll bet we would never have discovered it if . . ." But he did not have a chance to finish his sentence.

For at that moment a stream of ruby-red laser light flashed just above Osmyrrah's sleek back and left a small, smoking crater in the sand.

"What . . . ?" shouted William.

"Somebody's shooting at us!" yelled Maggie. "Hey! Stop it! Stop it!"

Another ray of deadly light zapped past them, even closer than before. William and Maggie dived into the sand. The third ray hit its mark, burning a long, black trail in Osmyrrah's silky fur. With a shrill whistle, Osmyrrah skittered off across the plain, leaving behind a new scent—the electric smell of terror.

"Don't shoot her!" screamed Maggie, leaping to her feet. "She's our friend."

"Get down!" cried William.

As he pulled her to the ground, a fresh blast of laser fire crackled past Maggie's head.

CHAPTER FOUR

The Smoky Top Report

MAGGIE PLUNGED INTO THE SAND BESIDE William, shielding her face against the sudden heat of the laser beam.

"Don't shoot!" cried William. "It's us—William and Maggie Murdock. Don't shoot!"

Maggie blinked dust from her eyes and searched the plain for signs of Osmyrrah. "Did they hit her? Where did she go?"

"Keep down," said William as another shot zapped past.

"But what if she's hurt?"

William shook his head. "She was running pretty fast. I think she's okay. What about you?"

"I'm all right. But why should anybody be shooting at us?"

At that moment the children heard a shout from beyond a distant, low dune. "William Murdock, is that you?"

"Yes! Yes! Don't shoot!"

A shaved head and meaty shoulders popped up from behind the hill. "It's me—Ludlow Brak. Is the monster gone?"

Maggie rolled her eyes and groaned. "Oh, no. Not Brak!"

Cupping his hands around his mouth, William shouted, "Yes, the monster's gone. Don't shoot."

He turned to Maggie and said with a wry smile, "I'm sure Councilor Brak meant well."

Maggie frowned and clenched her fists. "Well, *I'm* not so sure. Besides, it was a stupid thing to do. He could have killed us all."

William nodded. "Sometimes I wonder about him."

Maggie pressed her lips together and said nothing as she watched three colonists appear from behind the dune. "His creepy friends Zerski and Bilcher are with him, too. How did we get so lucky?" she grumbled.

Brandishing a lightpistol, Councilor Brak led the way toward the children. He was at least ten centimeters shorter than either of his companions. The sight of him clumping down the sand dune like a miniature bull, his bald head and spotless white clothes gleaming in the red sun, almost made Maggie laugh aloud. As it was, she clapped her hands over her mouth and snorted.

"Where have you children been? We've all been so worried about you!" Brak called, waving his pistol.

William got to his feet, helping Maggie up with

him. Maggie brushed sand and copperdust from her hands.

"We were lost in a copperdust storm, sir," said William.

Councilor Zerski lumbered through the sand to Brak's side, huffing and puffing. His jowly face wore an expression that made him look as if his breakfast had not agreed with him. "Really, children," he said sourly. "You led that monster right to our doorstep. I hope it doesn't come back with all of its friends to attack us."

"You don't understand, Councilor Zerski," said William. "She's not a monster. She's our friend. She saved us from dying in that copperdust storm."

Brak shook his head as he returned his lightpistol to its holster. His green eyes reflected the sun like two hard emeralds. "That's a hasty conclusion, my little friends. If that creature is what I think it is, we'd better be very careful."

"What do you mean?" said Maggie.

Brak laid a warm, slightly moist hand on her shoulder and gazed into her face as if he were her best friend. "I don't want to upset you, but I'm afraid the Smoky Top expedition has returned with rather frightening news. They've found evidence that this planet is inhabited by a very fierce race of spiderlike creatures."

Maggie's mouth dropped open. "But there must be some mistake," she said. "The spider we were with couldn't possibly be one of them. She saved our lives. She's a friend. An intelligent creature. She lives in a beautiful city in a crater full of grass and trees and animals, and her people want to communicate with us. They're *friendly.*"

"Oh, really?" said Brak, raising one eyebrow.

William frowned. "What kind of evidence did they find, sir? If you don't mind my asking."

"Why, of course not. Bilcher, my friend, do you still have that copy of the expedition's report?"

Bilcher grinned, proudly revealing an old-fashioned silver tooth. Maggie had heard that the tooth was an heirloom, and that Bilcher had inherited it from his father. He was as tall and lanky as Brak was short and square. The stubble of dark beard on his gaunt face gave him the look of a pirate.

"Yes, Luddy," he said in a voice too soft and pleasant to match his appearance. "I've got the report right here." He patted the breast pocket of his coveralls. Then, looking puzzled, he patted his hip and thigh pockets. "Well, I had it a minute ago," he mumbled.

Zerski scowled and made a soft clucking sound, then reached over and began to pat Bilcher's pockets himself. "Oh, for heaven's sake. Don't tell me you've lost it! Can't you do anything right, you dolt?"

Bilcher looked as if an obsidian hornet had stung him. "Everyone's allowed to make a mistake now and then," he said.

Brak waved his hand impatiently. "Well, it doesn't matter. The children can read a copy when we get back. Suffice it to say, William, that I find the evidence very convincing. It's hard to ignore a crater full of giant spiders, all apparently murdered in the same way."

William and Maggie exchanged astonished glances.

"But Councilor Brak . . ." William began.

"This isn't fair!" Maggie cried. "I don't care what they found. All I know is that Osmyrrah and her people wouldn't murder anybody."

Two small worry lines appeared on William's forehead. "At least not without a very good reason," he said.

"I'm sorry I had to shoot at the beast," said Brak. "But you can understand, I'm sure. From where we stood, it seemed clear that the creature was chasing you—with vicious intentions, I might add." Maggie caught the whisper of a satisfied smile on his ruddy face.

She had never liked Brak very much, even though he was a responsible and popular member of the New Genesis council. She hated the way he seemed to switch expressions as if they were no more than plastic masks. And she hated the way some people seemed to fall under his spell, almost against their own will.

"Well, Osmyrrah *wasn't* chasing us!" she found herself shouting. Blood roared like thunder in her ears. "You're the murderer! You're the one who tried to kill somebody!"

"Calm down, young lady," said Zerski, grabbing Maggie by the arm.

She jerked away, thrusting her chin out. "Don't touch me."

"Take it easy, Maggie," said William. "Brak was just trying to protect us. And anyway, people will soon find out there's no reason to fear the spider beasts."

Maggie rubbed at her sleeve where Zerski had touched it. "I hope so," she said, wondering if Brak had managed to beguile even her own brother. "But I know one thing for sure. Captain Stone's going to be pretty angry at you for taking potshots at Osmyrrah and us, Councilor Brak."

Brak shrugged and spread his hands apologetically. "I did what I thought was right, my dear. If Captain Stone is angry, I suppose it can't be helped."

Maggie felt like punching Brak, or screaming. She couldn't trust his fine speeches when the memory of Osmyrrah's pain and terror kept replaying itself in her head. With all the self-control she could muster, Maggie forced herself to turn around silently and begin walking through the sand toward Mount Jackson.

Brak pulled out a pocket communicator and used it to tell the other search parties, including William and Maggie's parents, that the children had been found. Then he and his friends and William joined Maggie in the march home.

As they trudged along the volcanic ash trail near the top of the cone, Maggie wondered what would happen when the colonists heard about Osmyrrah. Would they believe the children's story of friendship, or would they choose to believe Brak's frightening explanation of the Smoky Top report? She felt better when she thought about Captain Stone. She wished that all the councilors were like him. He had done a wonderful job of running the starship Genesis before they reached Earth II; and he was the only grown-up who had really believed in the Watchers even before William could prove the truth of his story. He had always been a good, wise friend to the children. Maggie felt confident that he would believe their story about Osmyrrah, too. But if people accepted Brak's version of things, Captain Stone wouldn't be able to do much about it. He was just another councilor now, better-liked than most, but with no more real power than any of the others.

Behind her, she heard Brak talking to William in cordial tones. "How's that wonderful sword of yours, William? Do you still have it?" he said. "You know, I've always admired what you and your amazing friends did for us on the Genesis. You're a very brave fellow."

William replied stiffly, "Thank you, sir. Yes, I still have Starnight. It's in a safe place."

There was an awkward pause. Then Brak said, "Well, that's good. And . . . how are things going for you and your family?"

"Things are going fine for us. Mom and Dad have been working hard on the crop projects, and Maggie and I try to help as much as we can whenever we're not in school. Dad says the soil's not as good as they'd hoped. The grain yields have been low so far, and we'll probably have to continue rationing next year."

"Yes, it's a shame, isn't it? If only Mount Jackson had turned out to be as fertile a place as we expected. But I suppose we're simply stuck with hard work unless we find a crater where farming is easier."

"I guess so," said William.

After a moment's silence Brak went on. "These spider beasts of yours . . . do they do much farming? Maybe we could learn something from them.''

At the mention of spider beasts, Maggie slackened her pace until Brak and William were walking beside her. Brak strutted along with his hands clasped behind his back and a charming grin on his face.

"It's hard to say whether they do much farming or not—they're so different from us," said William. "But their crater is beautiful. All kinds of things grow there.''

"Oh, really?" said Brak. "The soil must be wonderful. Much better than ours.''

William looked up at Brak and said slowly, "Maybe. But it's all native stuff. The native stuff always grows better than the things we brought from the Genesis.''

"Still," said Brak with a faraway look in his eyes. "We should find out whether their soil is better than ours." He glanced down at William, beaming as if he had just awakened from a pleasant dream. "Where is their crater, anyway?''

An electric spark of fear ran through Maggie. She squeezed William's arm hard and fairly shouted, "We don't know where it is.''

"That's right, sir," said William, flashing Maggie a wordless message of agreement. "We really don't know exactly where the spider beasts' crater is.''

Brak regarded the children with eyes narrowed almost to slits. "You can trust me, you know," he said.

William shivered visibly as he replied, "Of course,

sir.'' But though Brak waited, breathing loudly and impatiently, William said nothing more.

Before long, they stood at the top of the steep stairway that led down into the colony crater. The sun had only been up for a few hours, and soft morning light bathed Mount Jackson Valley. The Jubilation River meandered like a steaming snake from the north end of the crater to the south, flanked by fields and orchards. A cluster of reed houses and barns marked the town of New Genesis, nestled among the low hills near the river.

"Come along, children. I'm sure everyone is anxious to see you,'' said Brak, urging them forward.

Using explosives and high-intensity lasers, the colonists had carved a rough stairway into the igneous rock of the crater wall. Any day now, a new solar-powered elevator was to be put into operation. Until then, the stairs were the only way to get up and down the wall. The steps were steep and uneven, but William and Maggie often raced each other along them, heedless of danger.

"Well, what are we waiting for? Let's get going,'' said Maggie, with a wink.

William grinned, and before Brak, Bilcher, or Zerski even realized what was happening, the two children darted off down the stairs so nimbly that their feet barely seemed to touch the ground.

"Wait for us, confound you!'' shouted Zerski as he started down the stairs after them. But the children only laughed.

William and Maggie did not stop at the bottom. A

line of ground speeders stood at the foot of the stairway for the convenience of any colonist who wanted to use one. Fuel for the speeders was scarce and difficult to make, so the children usually walked the several kilometers from the stairs to New Genesis or caught rides on the produce sleds that sometimes passed by. But today was different.

"Come on," said William, hopping onto a speeder. "Let's go straight to Captain Stone's house. I think it's better if he hears our version of what happened before he hears Brak's."

William started the speeder, Maggie climbed on behind him, and they zipped away down the road to town.

Within a few minutes, they stood before Captain Stone's reed cabin on the edge of the New Genesis town square. A crowd of weary searchers had already gathered there to await the children's arrival. Among them were William and Maggie's parents.

"You two kids ought to be skinned alive for causing us all so much trouble and worry!" cried Mrs. Murdock, rushing to hug them both. Though her voice sounded stern and her thin, tan face wore a frown, she couldn't hide the tracks where tears of gladness had darkened the green dust on her cheeks.

The children's father bent to ruffle William's hair and kiss Maggie on the forehead. "Your mother's right," he said. "You should have been more careful. Goodness knows, we've got enough hard work to do here without having to comb half the planet for two overly adventurous kids."

"Sorry, Dad," said William.

"We didn't mean to get lost," said Maggie. "But wait till you hear our news!"

Just then Captain Stone himself trudged into the square. His bushy gray hair and eyebrows were covered with copperdust, for he, too, had been out with one of the search parties looking for the children.

"Captain Stone! Captain Stone! We've got to talk to you!" cried William.

"Well, William. Maggie. Where have you been? I hope you have a very good reason for causing us all this trouble," said the captain, shaking green dust from his shirt collar.

"We're sorry, sir. We got lost in a storm," said Maggie.

"Yes, sir. But that's not the important thing," said William.

"Out with it, my boy. We've a busy day ahead of us, you know. There's a field to be planted on the east side, and problems with the hydroelectric unit in section eighty-two."

"But, sir, we found aliens. Intelligent aliens," said William over the noise of the crowd of bystanders.

Silence fell on the town square. "Intelligent aliens? Alive?" said Captain Stone. "You're not talking about the dead ones we found at Smoky Top, are you?"

"No, sir. These are definitely alive. We made friends with one," said Maggie, shifting back and forth from one foot to the other. "Her name is Osmyrrah and she lives in a beautiful city by a river, and she talks with smells, and she and her friends can juggle crystal balls without even touching them!"

"Slow down, Maggie," said the captain, leaning toward the children. They could hear his breath catch with excitement. "Now, I want the two of you to tell me, very carefully and very slowly, exactly what you saw."

"But I already . . ." Maggie began.

William touched her arm. "I'll tell him."

Maggie bit her lip, angry at herself, convinced that the captain must think she was a baby. If only people would listen to *her* as they did to William.

She stood by in silence as William outlined their encounter with Osmyrrah and the other aliens. He told the story in a calm, clear voice, mentioning only what he and Maggie had seen, and not what they had thought.

"Friendly, intelligent aliens—not a stone's-throw away from us," said Captain Stone when William had finished. "Imagine what they might be able to teach us about this planet!"

"Captain, I'd like to contribute additional information, if I may," someone said in a loud, firm voice. Brak, who had just arrived from the stairway with Zerski and Bilcher, stepped through the crowd of colonists. "In point of fact, the beast's behavior looked ambiguous to us. I don't think it's really so clear that they're friendly and not just trying to trick us. Especially in view of the expedition's report about that mass grave at Smoky Top."

Maggie clenched her teeth and closed her eyes tight instead of kicking Brak in the shin as she wanted to. She nudged William and whispered, "The book. Show them the book. That'll prove the spider beasts are friendly and intelligent.''

"Wait a minute," said William. "Councilor Brak doesn't know about this." He opened his beltpack and removed the small shiny box, purposely holding it so the sun caught the crystal design on the top.

"Here," he said, handing it to the captain. "Our new friends gave us this."

The hushed colonists edged closer for a better look. Captain Stone opened the box and held up one of the black leaves. The white brush marks shone clearly on it. "Are you sure the creatures made this themselves?" he asked softly.

"Pretty sure, sir," said William.

The captain looked at Brak. "This seems to me like a pretty unambiguous sign of intelligence and a real desire to communicate with us on a friendly basis."

"Could I see that?" said Brak.

Bilcher reached down and grabbed Maggie by the back of the neck. He pulled her to one side so that Brak could get a better view of the box. She wiggled out of his grasp.

"Well . . ." said Brak. "It's not conclusive. It could still be a trick to gain our trust. Besides, I know what I saw. The monster fit the expedition's description of the bodies at Smoky Top. And it had its claws on Maggie when we arrived. There was no doubt in our minds that it intended to harm her, and *would* have if we hadn't frightened it off."

Maggie felt herself losing control of her temper again. She tried to stop herself, but it was no use.

"That's not fair, Councilor Brak. You know it's not!" she cried. "You make it sound like Osmyrrah was getting ready to kill me, and she wasn't. She was just touching me because she was happy. I wish you'd just leave us alone!"

"The child's just upset," said Brak, brushing nonexistent dust from his white jacket. "I can't blame her. What a terrifying experience she's had." He turned toward the crowd. "Fellow colonists, I urge you to beware. We cannot afford to trust these creatures until we know their true motives. We must proceed with caution, and be prepared to defend ourselves."

Cries and whispers ran among the colonists like the wind before a thunderstorm.

Brak waved his arms. "I think the first thing we should find out is the location of this city of spiders. And which direction an invasion would come from. We should at least be prepared for that."

"Invasion!" cried William. "But the only thing the spider beasts want is to be friends."

Brak moved his tongue around inside his cheek and grinned at William.

"Yes, my dear boy," said Councilor Zerski. "And I suppose their river flows with lemonade and their mountains are made of candy."

William clenched his fists. "Why are you doing this? Why can't you just believe us?"

Brak bent down and gazed into William's face. His kindly expression did not seem quite honest. "For your own safety and Maggie's, for the safety of your mother and father, for the safety of every colonist in Mount Jackson, that's why I'm doing it. For everyone's sake,

William—if you know where the city is, you must tell me.''

For an instant, Brak and William stared at each other with eyes as hard as laser crystals.

William's lips were almost white as he replied quietly, "No."

The kindly look evaporated from Brak's face. "It doesn't matter, William. We'll find out—one way or another," he said in a soft, terrible voice.

CHAPTER FIVE

The Meaning of Ozone

IN THE CONFUSION OF VOICES FROM THE crowd, no one heard Brak's threat except the children and Captain Stone.

The captain grasped Brak's arm and fixed him with a look as cold as deep space. "What are you trying to do, Brak? What gives you the right to harass these children?"

"What do you mean, harass?" said Brak, returning the captain's cool gaze with one of his own. "I am merely trying to ensure the safety of this colony by obtaining vital information from them." He pulled his arm from Captain Stone's grip.

The captain's cheeks colored slightly beneath his stubble of gray whiskers, and Maggie saw the muscles of his jaw tighten. For an awful moment, she wondered if there was going to be a fight.

But instead, Mrs. Murdock, who had watched the brief exchange with a puzzled frown, tapped

Brak on the shoulder. "I don't know exactly what this is about, Ludlow. But I think if my children have any vital information, they'll be able to relay it better after they've rested. I'm sure they're exhausted."

Brak glanced down at William and Maggie while momentary expressions of anger, frustration, and embarrassment flitted across his face. By the time he looked up at Mrs. Murdock again, he was wearing a gracious smile of apology.

"Of course," said Brak. "How thoughtless of me. By all means, we should wait till they've rested."

"Then Bill and I will take them home now, if it's all right." She tugged at Mr. Murdock's sleeve. He turned away from his conversation with one of the other crop foremen. Maggie saw her mother wink at him, the private signal they always used when one of them thought it was time to go.

Mr. Murdock smiled and extended his hand to Brak. "Thanks, Ludlow," he said. "I understand you're the one who found William and Maggie."

Brak beamed. "It was nothing, dear fellow. Nothing at all," he replied.

The children's father turned to Captain Stone. "You too, Max. We appreciate all your help."

"No problem," replied the captain. Hefting the spider beasts' shiny box thoughtfully, he turned to the children. "If it's all right with you, I'd like to give this alien book to one of the computer experts to see if we can translate it."

William and Maggie nodded their assent.

Mr. Murdock laid a firm hand on Maggie's shoulder. "Well, I suppose you two wouldn't mind some hot food and a nap, huh? Let's get home."

Waving, the four Murdocks left the town square and ambled toward their cabin, while the children, shouting and interrupting each other, told their parents all about Osmyrrah.

Maggie lay on her cot and looked up at the ceiling of her room. She had tried, but she couldn't go to sleep. It was afternoon—the wrong time for sleeping. Because of the planet's fifty-hour day, morning, afternoon, evening, and night each lasted over twelve hours. Though the colonists had tried at first, they soon discovered that no one had the stamina to stay awake for the twenty-five hours of daylight and then sleep for the twenty-five hours of darkness. To solve the problem, they had decided that afternoon and night should be set aside for waking, while morning and evening were for sleeping.

Besides the fact that she wasn't used to sleeping in the afternoon, Maggie was far too worried and excited to close her eyes. As soon as they arrived home, William and Maggie had used the household info-link terminal to print out a copy of the Smoky Top report. The words still burned through Maggie's thoughts like a laser beam.

"Most of Smoky Top's crater is occupied by a lake of molten lava. On the northeastern shore of this lake, however, we found traces of a highly intelligent (though probably extinct) alien race. We discovered the remnants of a city built primarily of crystal; in addition, we found what appears to be a vast open grave containing the corpses of thousands of huge spider or crablike creatures. The hard carapace of each creature appears to have been smashed in approximately the same place relative to the mandibles, with some heavy, blunt object. See sample 981M.''

Brak had been telling the truth about the report after all, and the evidence looked just as ominous as he said it did. Maggie felt certain the spider beasts would have a good explanation for it once they learned how to communicate, but there was no telling how the colonists would react in the meantime.

Maggie tossed and turned, wishing her mother and father hadn't had to leave for work. She wanted to talk and to be reassured that no one was going to hurt Osmyrrah. But as soon as the children had eaten, their parents had tucked them into bed and gone off to their jobs in the fields. ''It's a busy time right now,'' their mother explained. ''We're putting in wheat and lentils this week. We want to try a small crop of river nuts, too, and it just can't wait. We have to go and do what we can to help, but we'll be back by dusk.'' She had kissed them, and in a moment they heard the front door close behind her.

A warm, sweet breeze came through the window of Maggie's room, bringing with it the scent of freshly turned soil and the *clackety-clack* of seeding machines. Maggie had hung crystal slices on long strings from her ceiling. In the morning, just before she went to bed, the crystals sometimes caught the light of the rising sun and scattered it across the walls in little rainbows. Now they caught the breeze and tapped against one another with a soft, bright jingle. They reminded her of Osmyrrah's crystal house. One more time she thought of the beautiful alien city and of the kindness Osmyrrah had shown them.

When Maggie closed her eyes, she could almost see the spider beasts playing their juggling game in the steamy, turquoise river. The breeze whispered in through her window. *Clackety-clack* went the seeding machines; the crystal slices tinkled. Suddenly a distant shout and then another cut through the silk web of Maggie's daydream. She flung back her covers, hurried to the window, and looked out toward the sound of the voices. A knot of colonists milled about on the dusty road.

She ran to the door of William's room, but he was already up, gazing out through his own window.

"What's the ruckus about?" she asked, padding over to stand beside him.

"Don't know. Why don't we go see?" he replied, turning toward her eagerly.

The children tugged their coveralls back on and nearly knocked each other over as they ran for the front door. They were panting by the time they reached the gathering in the roadway. Breathless, William and Maggie stood on tiptoes on the fringes of the group, trying to see what the disturbance was about.

"It's Brak!" cried Maggie. "He's all beaten up!"

Ludlow Brak sat on a dusty ground speeder in the midst of the onlookers. His clothing was ripped and gaping in a dozen conspicuous places. A large, purplish bruise stood out on the shiny skin of his shaved head, and shallow pink scratches covered his cheeks.

High in one grimy hand, he held something that made Maggie gasp—the battered mandible of a spider beast!

"They attacked me for no reason. I had no choice," said Brak. "There must have been six or seven of them, roaring and howling, slashing at me. Their claws are sharp as razors."

William and Maggie stared at each other in horror. A cold, dark cloud of disbelief swirled around Maggie's head as she murmured, "That's impossible."

"I didn't want to shoot, of course. But they left me no choice. They'd have killed me. It was obvious," said Brak. His face was flushed and damp with perspiration. If he was lying, he was doing a very good job of it.

Still, Maggie found herself shouting, "They wouldn't *do* a thing like that! I can't believe it. And I wish you'd stop saying they have claws, because they *don't.*"

Brak shook his head and replied slowly, *"These* had claws. I'm afraid I've got the cuts and scratches to prove it."

Looking away, Brak dismounted stiffly from the ground speeder and, supported by two people from the crowd, limped off toward the infirmary. In twos and threes, the colonists began to disperse, returning to their interrupted tasks full of the news of an alien attack.

Before long, William and Maggie stood alone in the roadway, still too shocked to move.

"He's lying," said Maggie. "I don't think it's even *possible* for a spider beast to roar or howl.

And there's no such thing as a spider beast with claws.''

William ran his fingers through his hair. ''I don't know. Maybe we've just never seen one with claws. And how did he get all those scratches? *Something* happened to him.''

''You know the spider beasts as well as I do, William. You *know* they wouldn't do a thing like that, no matter what Brak says. I wouldn't be surprised if he tore his own clothes! And gave *himself* those scratches. He *could* have.''

''Yeah, but why would he want to? I don't see what he stands to gain by faking an alien attack.''

''I'm not sure yet,'' said Maggie. ''But I do know that he's trying as hard as he can to make people afraid of the spider beasts. And I also know I don't trust him to tell the truth about anything.''

''Yeah. It's pretty hard to believe they'd have hurt him.''

''I think we should go warn Osmyrrah that Brak's up to no good,'' said Maggie, jamming her fists into her hips. ''Who knows what he'll try to do next.''

William chewed at his bottom lip. ''But maybe they did attack him. Maybe they were upset because Brak shot at Osmyrrah. I wouldn't blame them. And if Brak did kill one of them just now, they're probably *really* upset.''

''Well, in that case, we should go and apologize to them. If we don't, they'll just get angrier and angrier. It's up to us. You know nobody else will do it.''

"Yeah," said William at last. "I guess you're right. Besides, I think we'd better figure out how to talk to them as fast as we possibly can. If we can communicate, things are less likely to get out of control. I want to take some language disks to them. Let's go get our stuff."

The children rushed around the cabin getting ready to go as swiftly as two of the purple-haired judabuckles that lived in the crags east of the river. Maggie stuck an emergency survival pack into one of the utility pockets in her overalls. William strapped on his beltpack and grabbed his pocket reader from its shelf by his cot. Placing it in the pack, he filled all the extra space around it with diskettes.

"Do you think the language diskettes will help them learn Spacers Standard?" asked Maggie.

"Well, I hope so anyway," said William.

"Are you going to take the sword, too?"

To Maggie's astonishment, William looked stunned for a moment, and then almost angry. "No. I'm not taking Starnight. I wish people would just forget about that sword, and the Watchers, too. Because I'm never going to call them again."

Maggie blinked, feeling surprised and puzzled. "What's the matter?" she said. "They told you they'd help you anytime, didn't they?"

"I just don't want to call them, that's all," William snapped.

The way he spat the words out made him seem like a stranger. Maggie shrugged off a sudden chill and said, "Suit yourself. You don't have to get mad."

With that, she opened the cabin door a crack to make sure there was no one passing by who might see them leaving. Startled at what she saw, she slammed the door closed again without meaning to.

"What's the matter?" said William.

"It's Bilcher! He's lying in the grass right outside our cabin, probably just waiting for us to leave. Goodness knows what he's planning."

William pressed his lips into a determined line. "Well, he'll be waiting a long time. Come on. We'll go out through one of the back windows."

The children ran straight to Maggie's window, crept through it, and raced into the adjoining field where the tall grass could hide them from Bilcher's view. They ran up the crater-wall stairs without stopping, then trotted down the packed ash trail on the outside of the volcano, resting only long enough to sip water from their canisters. They had not brought oxygen supplements, and the thin air of Earth II's surface slowed their progress across the plain toward the volcano cluster where they knew Osmyrrah's crater lay hidden. Though they weren't certain exactly where the cave entrance was located, they knew approximately which direction to head for. As they drew closer, some of the crystal formations and volcanic outcroppings began to look familiar, just as they had hoped. Two-and-a-half hours after they left Mount Jackson, they stood panting at the mouth of the passageway to the alien city.

The crystal cavern seemed just as awesome as before, its huge shafts of quartz eerily lit by the glowing rocks. Whenever they came to a branch in the tunnel,

Maggie closed her eyes and tried to remember which path was the right one. Though at times she had only a faint intuition to guide her, by and by she and William found themselves gazing down on the exquisite crystal city once again.

"See!" said William. "I told you it wouldn't disappear!"

Maggie took a deep breath as she and William started down the wide trail. For the first time, she began seriously to consider what might happen if Brak were telling the truth about having been attacked. Thinking about it made her jittery. After all, Brak had actually shot Osmyrrah with a lightpistol beam. She had a right to be angry. And if it were true that Brak had just killed a spider beast, even in self-defense, it was hard to say what kind of reception the children could expect in the alien city.

Well, thought Maggie, if they hate us, I can't blame them. And if they hurt us, it's our own fault. Still, somewhere deep inside, she could not imagine Osmyrrah hurting or hating anyone. It was this feeling that kept her going as they passed the star-topped trees and the pools where spider beasts played with the hovering balls, and strode through the soaring crystal archway to Osmyrrah's house. To Maggie's great relief, the creatures simply gazed at them as they passed, and made no move to stop them.

Osmyrrah greeted the children at her door, buzzing out blurry versions of their names and filling the air with the scents of roses and rain. The only sign of her confrontation with Brak and his laser beam was a shallow black trail through the fur of her carapace. Maggie sighed and patted Osmyrrah's back.

"We . . . we can't stay long," she said. "We've come to warn you. There's trouble."

"Maggie, I don't know how we can make her understand that," said William.

Maggie stood still for a moment, then said, "Smells! We'll tell her with smells!"

"Smells?" said William, wrinkling his forehead. "In the first place, we can't make smells as easily as Osmyrrah can. In the second place, we wouldn't know which ones to make, even if we could."

Maggie put her hands on her hips. "Don't be so sure, William Murdock. I know exactly which smell means danger."

"Well, if you're so smart, what is it then?"

"Remember when Brak was shooting at Osmyrrah? She made a smell just like the generators at the hydro-electric plant."

William frowned and gazed at Osmyrrah. "Gosh. I guess she did, didn't she. A sort of electrical smell . . . like . . . like . . . hey! I've *got* it! Ozone! That's it! Maggie, give me the survival kit."

Maggie tore at her pocket and brought out the small plastic box that contained their survival gear. "But, William, what's ozone?"

"It's a kind of gas—a special type of oxygen, I guess you'd say," said William as he flipped the lid open. "You get it when you expose oxygen to electricity or ultraviolet rays. That's why the generator smells that way. It's the ozone."

"But William—I don't get it. How's the survival kit going to help us?"

William held up a thumb-sized cylinder. "Do you know what this is?" he asked, grinning.

"Yeah. It's a water purification cartridge."

"Well, it's filled with ozone! They use ozone to purify water."

William and Maggie were about to hug each other in triumph when Osmyrrah began to buzz loudly and insistently.

"What is it?" said Maggie.

Osmyrrah pointed toward the top of the wide, steep trail that led from the cave mouth to the valley floor. There on the crystal shelf stood the compact figure of a man dressed in white.

Maggie's knees went weak. "It's Brak!" she whispered. The faint sounds of his laughter rode down to them on the fragrant breeze.

"What's he doing here?" cried William. "I thought he was on his way to the infirmary."

"I *told* you he was faking it," said Maggie. "He followed us! That creepy Bilcher must have seen us leave the cabin after all."

"Brak must have taken a ground sled to get here so fast. Captain Stone would be furious if he knew. There's hardly enough fuel to run the seeding machines, let alone ground sleds."

"Who cares how he got here? What'll we do?" A sick, empty feeling crept from Maggie's stomach to her throat.

William licked his lips. "All we can do is warn Osmyrrah now. But we'd better work fast."

He knelt down before the spider beast so that two of her great jet-black eyes were level with his own. Holding the purification cartridge before him, he pointed to Brak.

"That's Brak," said William. "He's dangerous." He pressed the release valve at the top of the cartridge. There was a soft hissing noise and a sudden smell of electricity as ozone escaped into the air. Osmyrrah jumped back as if startled. William closed the valve.

He repeated his actions. "Brak. Danger," he said, pointing; then he opened the valve and closed it again.

Osmyrrah chittered in agitation for a moment. Then she raised one of her front legs toward Brak and said in her buzzing, raspy voice, "Brak. Danger."

Maggie sniffed the air. "Ozone!" she exclaimed. "I think Osmyrrah's got the message."

William nodded as they watched Brak retreat into the crystal cavern. "Good," he said. "Because it looks like he's headed back to New Genesis, and I think we'd better be right behind him. Who knows what he might try to do, now that he knows where the city is."

William fumbled with the flap on his beltpack and took out the pocket reader and the book diskettes.

"Here, Osmyrrah. I'll show you how this works," he said, inserting a diskette into the scanner slot. The little machine hummed softly. Several lines of writing appeared in black against the reader's light blue screen. With the flick of a switch, the lines moved slowly upward at easy reading speed. The machine's mechanical voice read aloud at the same pace. Osmyrrah watched with interest, emanating a smoky scent like burning leaves, her hinged mandibles clicking slightly.

"These are *books*, Osmyrrah. *Books,*" said William, pressing the reader and diskettes into Osmyrrah's sticky-tipped tentacles. "Read them. Maybe they'll help you understand us. Believe me, we've got a lot of questions to ask."

He shook his head and smiled at Maggie. "I don't know why I'm always talking to her. I guess I just wish she could understand, you know?"

Maggie nodded in agreement, then said softly, "Come on, William. We'd better get going. You're right about Brak." She turned to Osmyrrah and patted her furry back again to say good-bye. "So long, Osmyrrah. We have to go now. Be careful."

William waved as they started up the obsidian trail. "Good-bye, Osmyrrah! Good-bye!"

Just as they ran through the crystal archway, the children heard Osmyrrah call, "Good-bye, William. Good-bye, Maggie."

William and Maggie spoke hardly at all as they trudged back across the plain. The long hours of daylight were almost over, and the sun hung like a ripe persimmon near the horizon. No breeze stirred the air. Only the plume of steam from distant Smoky Top marred the emptiness of the landscape. The sky stretched over the children like a crystal bowl, ruby and emerald along the rim, black as obsidian above their heads. It seemed to them that darkness was descending on all they had hoped for.

Partway up the trail to Mount Jackson crater, they stopped to catch their breath. Maggie leaned against a boulder, rubbing the sore muscles in her legs, wondering how many kilometers they had walked altogether since dawn.

William stared pensively toward Osmyrrah's volcano. "I think Brak must be lying about that attack. If he had really killed one of them, the aliens would be upset about it. I know they would. But instead they act as if nothing's happened. It's crazy. I can't believe the spider beasts would ever have hurt him. He doesn't act like he's afraid of them, and you'd think he *would* be afraid, if he's telling the truth."

Maggie sniffed. "He's lying all right. That business about the claws is enough to convince me. This time, I purposely looked for a spider beast with claws. I didn't see a single one. And you're right. Brak's not really afraid of them himself. He's *got* to be lying."

"But I can't figure out why he should lie about a thing like that," said William.

"I'll bet he wants something," said Maggie angrily. "He's such a bully he's willing to do *anything* to get whatever it is. I wish he would just grow up, and stop making things hard for everybody else."

"Oh, come on, Maggie. He's as old as Mom and Dad. He *is* grown-up."

"I'm not so sure," said Maggie, tossing her head. "I heard Mom say once that there's more to being grown-up than just having an old body."

Still wondering what it was that Brak could possibly be after, the children made their weary way down the crater-wall stairs and across the valley to New Genesis just as dusk fell. They saw no sign of Brak. By the time their parents returned from the fields, William and Maggie lay wrapped in their blankets, fast asleep, as if they had been there for many hours.

CHAPTER SIX

Traitors

IT WAS STILL DARK WHEN MRS. MURDOCK called the children from their dreams.

"Time to get up, kids," she announced from the hallway. "It's almost twenty-five o'clock. You'll be late for school."

Maggie sat up on her cot and groaned. She ached all over from the walking she had done the day before, and she felt as if she'd hardly slept at all. "Aw, Mom, can't I stay home today?" she mumbled. "I'm still tired."

Mrs. Murdock came to the door of the room. She stood straight and tall, her slender body perfectly balanced, a smile on her tan face. "No room for lazybones in New Genesis, sweetie. You've had plenty of sleep." She clapped her hands. "Now scat! Get washed up. Breakfast's waiting."

Maggie gulped back the protest she was about to make as she remembered that her mother didn't know about their second trip to the alien city. She dragged herself wordlessly to the bathroom and almost fell asleep in the geothermal shower. William banged on the door, shouting for her to hurry up. At breakfast, she spooned grape-apple preserves onto a thick slice of Jubilation mushroom and thought of absolutely nothing while she chewed it.

Mr. Murdock scanned the info-link screen as he ate. "Hmm," he said between bites of crisp fried skyfish. "Looks like they'll have the solar elevator working sometime today or tomorrow. What a time-saver that'll be." He pressed a button, and the information on the screen moved up slowly. "They've called for a council meeting at dawn. Probably to debate this suggestion of Luddy Brak's."

"What suggestion?" said William.

"Yeah! What suggestion?" Maggie echoed as Brak's name cut through her dream fog.

"He and some of the other councilors think it might be a good idea to set up laser artillery on the crater rim. Didn't you hear the news? Brak was attacked by aliens yesterday out on the plain."

"Of course we heard. But laser artillery! That's crazy!" cried Maggie, springing out of her seat.

"Finish your breakfast," said her father, frowning. "It's not crazy at all. As a matter of fact, it makes good sense, in light of what's happened."

"But, Dad . . ."

Mr. Murdock raised his eyebrows. "You certainly got up on the wrong side of the bed this morning. Settle down and eat now."

Maggie knew better than to argue with her father when he spoke in such a firm tone of voice. But the Jubilation mushroom that had seemed so good a moment before tasted worse than frog skin after the news of Brak's suggestion.

Her blood still fizzed with anger as she and William gathered their school diskettes and notebooks and walked out into the darkness. Though dawn would not arrive for a long while yet, life in the colony went on almost as if the sun shone brightly. School started at twenty-six o'clock, just after midnight. The road was already busy with colonists embarking on a new day's work.

All three of the planet's moons hung in the green-black sky. Their combined red and golden light washed across the cinder road as Maggie kicked every pebble she came to. "Laser artillery!" she grumbled. "You'd think we were at war or something. If Brak keeps up like this, somebody's really going to get hurt. Then we'll *never* be able to make friends with Osmyrrah's people."

"I'll bet he's going to discuss more than laser artillery at that council meeting at dawn," said William. "He's probably going to try to make himself look like a hero by announcing the location of the spider beasts' crater."

Maggie stopped in the middle of the road, her eyes wide. "Oh, William!" she cried. "What if they decide to attack the spider beasts?"

"I don't think they will. Not yet anyway. Luckily, most people have more sense than Brak. But I do think we ought to go to that meeting and make sure everybody hears the other side of the story."

"I hope you're right," said Maggie, kicking another pebble as she started to walk again.

Beside her, William stared into the distance. "There's something scary going on," he said, almost as if he were talking to himself. "Something we haven't figured out yet. I don't like the questions Brak was asking yesterday. Nosy questions about the soil in Osmyrrah's crater. And about Starnight." A shiver ran through him. Maggie saw goose bumps rise on his arms and neck. When he turned to look at her, the moonlight made dull red sparks in his eyes. "I'm afraid, Maggie," he said. "I'm afraid he wants Starnight, and that he wants to do something terrible with it."

Maggie felt his fear squirming its way into her own bones. She walked closer to him. "You shouldn't worry about that," she said, hoping she sounded brave and confident. "You know it's impossible for him to steal Starnight, even if he really does want it. Even if you're not just imagining things."

William shook his head. "He wants it, all right. Don't ask me how I know. I can just tell."

"So what? He can't steal it. So why worry?"

"Because he'll try. You know how he is. He'll try anyway."

Before long, the children arrived at the New Genesis schoolhouse, a low, spacious building made of river reeds and clay. William and Maggie reached their places just in time to sing "The Anthem of the Generation Ship" along with the rest of the class. Usually, Maggie liked the song. But this morning it just made her feel gloomy. She thought longingly of the old steel-walled classroom aboard the starship Genesis. She remembered the steady low vibration of the ship's turbines, and the damp, chemical smell of recycled air. Life was simple and straightforward aboard the starship. Sometimes she wished they had never landed on this planet, where there were so many dangers and so many ways to get into trouble. But it was no use. The Genesis orbited Earth II like a little moon now, airless and abandoned. The sight of it traveling across the night sky would always be a reminder to the colonists. They were lucky to be here and lucky to be alive, no matter how hard things seemed on the new planet.

When the song was over, the children sat down in front of their info-links. The teacher remained standing.

"Class, I have a special announcement to make before we begin today," said Mr. Masataka, his thick dark hair gleaming in the muted light from the ceiling globes. "The council met yesterday, and they have made a suggestion which they've asked me to pass on to you."

Maggie leaned across the aisle. "I'll bet this is another one of Brak's ideas," she whispered to William.

"As you know, intelligent aliens have recently been discovered living in a nearby volcano cone similar to ours," said Mr. Masataka.

Whispers rustled through the classroom.

"Yesterday, a band of aliens attacked Councilor Ludlow Brak while he was out on the plain. He was forced to protect himself with a lightpistol, and unfortunately one of the aliens was killed."

At the word "killed," the room became so quiet that Maggie could hear the distant rush of the Jubilation River.

"Since we really know very little about these aliens, and since their actions indicate that they may be warlike, the council has strongly recommended that all colonists stay off the plain and inside the crater until further notice."

"But, Mr. Masataka!" Maggie cried.

Mr. Masataka frowned at her and said, "Please do not speak out of turn, Maggie."

Maggie crossed her arms and stuck her lip out but managed to keep quiet. It infuriated her to think of the council's asking people to stay off the plain when they ought to be busy making friends with the spider beasts instead. It seemed clearer and clearer that Brak was doing everything in his power to cause friction between the colonists and the aliens. She was so angry at this terrible news that she hardly heard another word the teacher said until he clapped his hands for recess.

William and Maggie left their seats and jostled through the door with the other children.

Maggie leaned close to William's ear. "They can make me weed vegetable patches from now till doomsday," she whispered. "But I'm not going to stay off the plain, and I'm not going to stay away from Osmyrrah."

"Neither am I," said William. "It just makes me more certain than ever that we'd better go to that council meeting and try to stop Brak once and for all."

As they stood on the playground in the bluish light of the field lamps, someone tapped William on the shoulder. It was Josh Wedekind, Ludlow Brak's nephew, older than William by two years. A group of his friends stood behind him.

"Is it true that you know where the alien city is and you refused to tell the council?" said Josh. The set of his jaw betrayed the fact that he was angry and ready for a fight.

"Look, Josh. I refused to tell Ludlow Brak where the city is because I don't trust him. The *council* never asked me. Anyway, it doesn't matter anymore."

Josh clenched his fists and held his arms bent at the elbows. "What do you mean, it doesn't matter? You should have told the council whether they asked you or not. *I* think you're a sneaky little traitor, and your sister, too. You're gonna get us all killed. Did you stop to think about that?"

Maggie could almost see the adrenaline rushing through William's veins as he thrust out his chin and brought up his own fists. "If anybody's going to get us killed, Josh Wedekind, it's your stupid uncle."

Luckily, Mr. Masataka walked up just then. He laid one hand on William's shoulder and one hand on Josh's. "All right, boys. Fighting won't solve anything."

Josh spat on the ground at William's feet and turned away without another word. His friends followed him, giving William backward glances of disgust.

William and Maggie, like all the children of New Genesis, had chores to do after school. Running errands and helping with weeding or harvesting were not always what they wanted to be doing after a day of classes. But Mount Jackson crater was certainly no paradise. They understood how hard it was to grow enough food and produce enough energy for the colony's needs. Today, instead of going straight home from the reed schoolhouse, they spent a few hours helping to clean and sort a catch of skyfish from the river.

Thoughts of Osmyrrah and laser artillery played over and over in Maggie's mind as she sorted through the cold, coppery fish in the half-light from two electric globes. Her eyes burned and her head ached by the time she and William returned to their cabin to change clothes and get ready for the council meeting.

They were surprised to find the door standing open and their mother talking to two men who wore security-duty armbands. Several neighbors and a couple of councilors, including Ludlow Brak, were wandering through the rooms, stopping here and there to peer closely at the floors and walls.

Mrs. Murdock flicked back a strand of her light brown hair with impatient fingers. "No, I didn't see anything," she told the security men. "When I got home, the cabin was just as you see it—the door wide open and things scattered all over the place. We've never had any crime in New Genesis before. Who would do such a thing?"

"I don't know, ma'am. We'll have to examine the cabin and see if we find any clues."

"Hey, what's going on?" said Maggie.

"I'll tell you what's going on," said Brak from the far corner of the living room. Maggie couldn't quite see what he grasped delicately in his fingertips. "This house has been ransacked by aliens. Here's the proof."

He strode over and placed several short, thick hairs in the palm of one of the security men. "Hair from the carapace of a spider beast. I can identify it beyond any doubt."

"Let me see," said William.

The security man lowered his hand so the children could get a better look. Maggie heard the breath whoosh out of her brother as if he'd been hit in the stomach. It was definitely the hair of a spider beast.

"I don't believe it!" she cried. "There's nothing in our cabin that a spider beast would want to steal."

Brak crossed his stubby arms on his chest and said, "What about the sword?"

Maggie couldn't have felt worse if she had swallowed a large, cold brick. Staring at William in horror, she said thinly, "Maybe we'd better look."

Brak bent down to gaze into the children's faces. Maggie drew back, suddenly feeling as if the furrows of concern in Brak's forehead were made of glass. Beneath them lurked something else—a look of terrible anticipation and greed. "Yes, my little friends. Maybe you'd better go see," he said.

"Starnight's in . . . in a safe place," William stammered. "I'm not worried."

Anger fluttered briefly across Brak's face before he regained his expression of kindly concern. "I really do think it would be a good idea to check."

"I'll . . . I'll check later," said William.

But Brak persisted. "That sword is practically a New Genesis colony treasure, after all."

At that, Mrs. Murdock, who had been watching with a frown, tapped Brak on the shoulder. She flashed him the same wide, strained smile she sometimes used on the children when they were about to get into trouble. ''He told you he'd check later.''

Brak stood up quickly, looking huffy and vaguely ruffled. ''Quite so,'' he said and stamped out of the cabin into the dark road beyond.

As soon as he was gone, Maggie whispered, ''Come on. Let's go check Starnight.''

But William shook his head. ''Can't you see that's just what Brak wants us to do? He's probably standing outside right now, peeking through the window, hoping we'll show him right where Starnight's hidden.''

''But what if it's been stolen?''

''The spider beasts don't even know that sword exists. I'd bet a year's ration of sugar that Brak planted those hairs in here to cover up the fact that he's the one who ransacked our cabin. He was probably looking for Starnight.''

''Okay!'' said Maggie, struggling to keep her voice down. ''But what if he found it? What if it's gone?''

''We still have to wait a while,'' said William. ''But try not to panic. It's probably still safe in its hiding place. You know as well as I do that Starnight won't let anyone touch it except you and me.''

Maggie began to breathe again as she remembered the sword's magical ability to keep people from touching it. ''All right, all right,'' she said. ''But I'll feel a lot better when we've made sure.''

After the excitement had died down, William and Maggie slid the cabin's window covers into place and rushed into William's room. William ran straight to his closet, opened it, and reached between neatly hung coveralls and tunics. Carefully, he felt for the spring latch of the secret compartment built into the back wall. The hidden door slid back.

There lay Starnight, its massive hilt pulsing with orange-and-white light, its wondrous blade concealed by a long leather sheath. William reached toward it, grasped the glowing handle, and slid the sword from its sheath. It pulsed eerily as it lay in his arms. First orange, then white, engraved pictures of strange creatures and nameless landscapes ran from the hilt to the needle-sharp tip of the blade.

Maggie let her breath out slowly. "Thank goodness," she said.

William slid the sword back into the sheath and replaced it in the hidden compartment. "I've always had the feeling we'd someday be very glad we built this hiding place." He smiled triumphantly.

Maggie nodded, still too shaken to share William's good spirits. "I just hope it keeps working," she said. "Now if only the council will believe what we're going to tell them. We'd better hurry, or we'll be late."

With an empty feeling, Maggie watched William as he sat stiffly on a chair in the front of the council hall. He looked fidgety and uncomfortable in his best coveralls. Maggie couldn't decide whether she was glad she wasn't in his place or angry because he had insisted she keep silent and let him do all the talking.

The whole thing reminded her too much of their last appearance before the council. Aboard the Genesis, she and William had tried to convince the councilors that the Watchers of Space were real. All it had gotten them was an official reprimand and five weeks worth of weeding duty on the ship's vegetable farm. She crossed her fingers and hoped things would go better this time.

"Now, William," said Captain Stone. "Since you and your sister were the first colonists to have contact with the aliens, we'd like you to tell us a little bit about what happened. How did they treat you, for example? And what do you think of them?"

Zerski snorted loudly from his seat behind the long council table. "I'm sure we all know what the children think of them. Why should we concern ourselves with a child's innocent trust of such dangerous creatures?"

Councilor Brak looked back and forth from Zerski to Captain Stone, half grinning as he said, "Nonsense, Councilor Zerski. In New Genesis, everyone's entitled to be heard. I'm sure our young friend's opinions will be very helpful."

William swallowed hard. "We were lost in a copperdust storm," he said, looking straight at Brak. "One of the spider beasts found us and led us to shelter. They took care of us until the storm passed. If it hadn't been for them, we'd probably be dead right now. They didn't have to save us. I'm positive they want to be our friends, and I don't understand why Councilor Brak won't believe us."

"The evidence suggests that they don't want to be our friends at all," said Brak.

The lines in Captain Stone's forehead deepened with anger as he said, "Let the boy finish."

Brak stood up and clasped his wide hands behind his back. "I beg your pardon, Councilor Stone. But the boy is obviously finished already if this is all he can tell us. He's clearly been duped.'' He narrowed his eyes as he held up a finger and said with great relish, ''One: I had to defend the children from their alien 'friend' myself when we initially found them. It seemed clear to me that the beast was prepared to attack them.'' He raised another finger. ''Two: I myself was attacked by aliens shortly after that.'' Another finger. ''Three: Their city does not show up in any of the orbital survey photos we've taken. Regardless of how they've managed this, I'd like to ask one question: If their intentions are so honorable, why have they been hiding from us?''

He slapped both of his hands down on the table before him. ''Add to this the fact that the Murdocks' cabin has just been ransacked by a spider beast which left obvious signs of itself in nearly every room! Give me one good reason for trusting such creatures,'' he shouted.

Maggie leaped to her feet, unable to keep silent any longer. ''You're nothing but a liar, Ludlow Brak!'' she screamed. ''You made all of this up. I'll bet no alien ever attacked you. I'll bet you just wanted it to look that way! And you're the one who ransacked our cabin. Stop it! Stop it! Stop it!'' Maggie tried to climb over the table to reach Brak. She felt like punching him in the nose. But strong hands held her securely.

She twisted around and found herself staring into her father's face. ''Settle down, Maggie,'' he said quietly.

Brak looked a little flustered as he glared at Maggie. He was plucking nonexistent lint from his spotless white clothes again, a thing he only did when he was upset. "Your accusations are preposterous," he said, spitting each word out like a separate blast of laser fire.

But as Maggie watched the way his hands jerked across the immaculate folds of his jacket, certainty washed over her in a powerful wave. She was right. Everything she had said was right.

CHAPTER SEVEN

The Desperate Plan

MAGGIE KICKED AND SHOUTED AS HER father and one of the other colonists dragged her from the council hall. "It's not fair!" she cried. "He's lying. Don't believe him!"

But no one would listen.

When William, too, had been escorted from the hall, Mr. Murdock stood outside the door holding each of them by an arm. "I'm ashamed of you," he said to Maggie. "How could any child of mine behave so inexcusably?"

"But, Dad!" said Maggie. "You told us we should never put up with a liar. And Councilor Brak is lying."

"You don't know that, Maggie. It's just something you want to believe. You have judged him unfairly, and I'm ashamed of you."

If her father's words had been made of fire, they could not have burned any worse. Maggie's eyes stung, and she tried to swallow the aching in her throat.

"Now I want both of you to go home and go to bed." He gave them a little push. "Go on. Get out of here."

Numbly, the children stumbled down the moonlit steps into the road. Behind them, they heard the door close as their father went back into the hall.

William tugged at Maggie's sleeve.

"What?" she snapped, swiping at the tears of hurt and anger that had slid down her cheeks.

"I want to find out what they decide," said William. "Let's go hide under one of the windows."

Maggie shrugged, too injured to speak or even to care very much what else was said in the council hall.

She let William shepherd her to one of the windows, and she crouched beside him in the shadows as he listened.

"All those in favor of raising an army of defense," someone said.

There was a loud chorus of "aye"s.

"Those opposed?"

The lonely voice of Captain Stone drifted through the window. "No."

William pulled Maggie to her feet. "Come on," he said. "We don't need to hear any more."

Maggie stumbled along behind him as he hurried onto the road and jogged off toward their cabin. She felt like a wooden doll. "It's my fault," she mumbled. "It's all my fault."

"Oh, for Pete's sake, Maggie!" said William. "Snap out of it, will you? So you made a scene. It doesn't matter. We never would have convinced them anyway."

"Do you really think so?" Maggie asked hopefully.

"Of course I do."

"But what do we do now? Everything's in a terrible mess."

"We go and warn Osmyrrah, that's what. It's our only chance of stopping this."

"But . . . but people already think we're traitors," said Maggie, panting with the effort of keeping up with him. "If we run off and tell the spider beasts all of the council's plans, that's really going to look good."

"I don't care," said William. He stopped abruptly in the road. Moonlight washed across his face, rigid with determination. "Think about this. If the spider beasts can hide their city from orbital cameras, if they can make balls of crystal float just by looking at them . . . why couldn't they disintegrate an army just by looking at it?"

Maggie stared as William's words sank in. Vivid pictures began to form in her mind—first of Brak using his lightpistol to cut off Osmyrrah's mandibles, then of every colonist on Earth II disappearing in a puff of leaden smoke.

"Great spacefire!" she whispered harshly. "Let's get going."

The children stopped at their cabin only long enough to change into survival coveralls and grip boots and to fill their beltpacks. They plumped fluffy reed-top pillows beneath the blankets on their cots in hopes of fooling their parents into thinking they were asleep.

As they were about to leave, Maggie touched William's arm and said, "What about Starnight? Shouldn't we take it along?"

William rummaged busily in his beltpack as he shook his head.

"But will it be safe here? What if Brak finds it while we're gone?" Maggie asked.

"It's safer here than it would be with us," said William, closing the pack and buckling it around his waist.

"Are you sure?"

"Stop nagging me about it! Starnight stays here. Now let's get going."

Maggie rolled her eyes as she buckled on her own pack and followed him out into the predawn darkness.

They crept through the grass beside the road, heading toward the crater-wall stairs, flattening themselves against the ground whenever they saw someone coming. The stairway itself seemed deserted. It lay in the deep shadow of the waning moons, invitingly dark.

"Look," said William, pointing to the new metal track that ran up the wall. "We're in luck! They've got the solar elevator working. That means the stairs will probably be deserted."

It was no time at all before William and Maggie stood in the shadow of a boulder at the top of the stairs, watching as the first light of dawn brightened the eastern horizon. Hugging the sheltered cliff face, they hurried down the trail toward the crystal plain and the cluster of volcanoes in which Osmyrrah's crater lay.

As they trotted along, Maggie took a deep breath. A dozen times since Josh Wedekind had accused them of being traitors, she had thought of Orion and Starnight, and stopped herself from blurting one simple question. But now she was certain the time had come to ask it.

"William, the Watchers said they'd always be your friends, didn't they?" She gestured toward his hand, where the Watchers' silver spot glowed like a luminous diamond. "That's the proof. They wouldn't have given you that sign unless they really meant it. It would be so easy for them to straighten all of this out. Why haven't you called them?"

William refused to look at her, but she could see the tightness she had expected in his face. His voice quavered slightly as he said, "Things are going to have to get a lot worse than this before I'll even consider calling the Watchers. So just forget it."

Maggie knew from the tone of his voice that she ought to drop the subject before he got angry. But the terrible thought of colonists and spider beasts in armed combat drove her on. She took one more deep breath and said, "William, please tell me what this is all about. It's not fair to me. And it's not good for you to just keep it all inside you like this. What happened? Why don't you want to call the Watchers? Did they do something awful to you? You almost act like you're afraid."

In the moonlight, the little twitch that ran across his face was faint but unmistakable. He turned away and stared into the distance. "No. It's nothing they did to me. Just something that happened. You're right, I guess. I'm afraid."

"But why?"

"Cygnus," William replied softly.

Maggie scratched her head and squinted at him.

"Who's Cygnus? You've never mentioned him before."

William stopped abruptly in the middle of the trail.
"Mentioned *her*. I never mentioned *her* before. And
the right question is, Who *was* she?" He kicked a pebble so hard that it raised shining motes of greenish dust
in the moonlight. He shoved his hands into his pockets
and began walking again.

"What do you mean?" said Maggie.

William stared at the road before them. She could
see him blinking hard, and his eyes were too bright.
"She's dead." His voice was almost a whisper.

Maggie had seen William in all kinds of trouble before. She had seen him smile through a hundred bruises
and skinned knees. She had seen him take a reprimand
from the council with a calm face and square shoulders.
She had seen him stand up for his rights even when his
pride was hurt. But she had never seen such a look of
pain about him as she saw now.

She knew she ought to say something, but she didn't
know what, for she hadn't had much experience with
death. She had thought about it a little, before William
saved the starship and it looked like all the colonists
would die in space. But even then, she had never really
believed it would happen. She had never known anybody who died. All she really knew about death was
that she hated it when her pet judabuckles died. Now
she tried to imagine a much bigger sadness. It frightened her.

"I should have told you before, I guess," said William, still looking down at the road. "While I was
missing from the Genesis all that time . . . I wasn't

just running around looking for the special stones
Orion said we could use for fuel. Finding them wasn't
the problem. It was *getting* them that was hard. They
were guarded by a monster—the Unhappy One. Before
I could get the stones, I had to kill the Unhappy One,
with Starnight. It was the scariest thing I've ever
done.''

"But I don't understand. What does that have to do
with this Cygnus person?" Maggie asked softly.

"You see, I didn't fight the monster all by myself.
There was a Watcher with me. The kindest, most beautiful Watcher of all. Cygnus. The Unhappy One killed
her. She was trying to save me.''

Maggie thought in silence for a long time. She tried
to think of herself in his place. After a while, she said,
"If she *wanted* to save you, then maybe it wasn't your
fault she died.''

William only shrugged. Maggie could see that he
didn't really believe what she had said.

From the jumble of feelings inside her, the most familiar ones emerged: impatience and a little anger.
"I'm sorry she died, William. I'm sorry you got hurt.
But you know, you can't let that stop you from doing
what's right. You'd better think about that. Because if
we can't stop Brak by ourselves, and you can't bring
yourself to call the Watchers, a *lot* of people are going
to die.''

With that, she marched ahead, grinding the heels of
her boots into the ashen trail at every step. Though she
felt sure she was right, she hated what she had said and
the way she had said it.

She was still a little ahead of him when they reached

the crystal plain, but their trek continued uneventfully. They kept close to boulders and crystal formations as much as they could, and if anyone saw them, there was no sign of it. Before long, William and Maggie were following the faintly lit tunnel passage to the wide rock shelf above Osmyrrah's city.

Halfway down the trail to the valley, a group of three spider beasts approached them. Maggie sniffed the air. "Peaches. A forest. Roses and rain! It must be Osmyrrah and her friends."

"Hello, Maggie. Hello, William," the spider beasts buzzed in chorus.

"They're speaking Spacers Standard!" She flashed William a grin and was relieved when he answered it with a small one of his own.

"We have read the book disks," said the one who smelled like peaches.

"But that's amazing," said Maggie. "How did you learn so fast?"

The spider beasts clicked their mandibles and jiggled their bodies from side to side. A pungent scent like peeled cucumbers rose from them.

Osmyrrah said, "We are . . . laughing. Is that the word? My nestparent and my waterparent say you must think we are . . . not very smart?" The three spider beasts clicked and jiggled and a fresh whiff of cucumbers rose up.

"Oh," said William, his cheeks suddenly rosy. "Oh, we didn't mean that at all!" He glanced toward Maggie, grimacing. "We meant that you're much smarter than we are. Our computer people are still try-

ing to figure out that book you gave us. I mean—we
haven't learned *your* language yet.''

"But we *want* to," said Maggie. "Oh, Osmyrrah!
We want to learn everything about you. We want to be
your friends. But everything is so mixed up." She
thought of the council meeting and of how Brak was
probably raising an army at this very minute, and she
swallowed without intending to. "We've got to stop
Brak!"

"What is wrong?" buzzed the one who smelled like
a forest.

William looked distressed. He glanced worriedly at
Maggie, then back at the spider beasts. "Brak has
made people afraid of you. He's been saying things.
That a spider beast attacked him and he had to kill it in
self-defense. That a spider beast sneaked into New
Genesis and ransacked our cabin."

Osmyrrah produced a smell like burning leaves. "I
do not understand. No one has been killed. No one has
been to New Genesis."

Maggie felt like hugging Osmyrrah. The only reason
she didn't was that she was afraid it might offend the
spider beasts. "I knew it!" she cried. "I knew Brak
was making up the whole thing. I bet the councilors
will change their minds now!"

But William shook his head. "It's not enough, Maggie," he said. "Even if Osmyrrah told the council what
she just told us, they probably wouldn't believe her.
Where did Brak get those mandibles if he didn't kill a
spider beast, for example? And why were there traces
of spider beasts in our cabin? No matter how certain it
seems to us that Brak's lying, the council's going to

want more proof than you and I and Osmyrrah can give them right now.''

Maggie hated the wave of desperation that rose inside her. She fought it with anger. ''Well then, what are we supposed to do? Why did we even bother to come here at all?''

William looked away, across the lush valley to the far crater wall, then back at Maggie. ''I think the only thing we can do is warn them, Maggie. Do you want to tell them what's happened, or shall I?''

Maggie stood without speaking for an instant, her hands clenched at her sides. Then she turned to the three spider beasts. ''They're installing laser artillery on the rim of Mount Jackson. They've decided to organize an army. And I'm afraid, Osmyrrah. I'm afraid that before long, Brak will find some excuse to lead them in an attack against you.''

For a long, long moment, the spider beasts made no sound at all. They stood as if frozen in their heavy shells, while a sad and overwhelming smell poured from them—the sweet tang of river reeds when the season's first rains come. It was Peaches and Forest who finally broke the silence with a concert of buzzes and clicks in their own language. Osmyrrah soon joined in the noisy chorus. Complex patterns of smells rose from them as they communicated. The children could not say for certain, but it seemed to them that the spider beasts were arguing over something.

Minutes passed as slowly as hours while William and Maggie waited to see what would happen. Suddenly, the clicks and buzzes stopped. Peaches and Forest wheeled about and scuttled away in the direction of the river without a word to the children. The faint, sharp smell of ammonia hung about Osmyrrah like a halo, mixed with the scent of ozone.

"The one you call Peaches, my nestparent, and the one you call Forest, my waterparent, will not listen to me. They have gone to call a meeting of the pools. They say the time has come to join our mindpatterns into the ancient weapon."

"Mindpatterns? The ancient weapon?" said William. "What's a meeting of the pools?"

"I do not know enough words to explain well," said Osmyrrah. "Mindpatterns are the energy formed by the joining of our thoughts. Mindpatterns do many things. They helped us learn Spacers Standard quickly. They power our bubble ships. They helped us hide our city from your cameras. But they do other things as well.

"It is written in the Leafbox of Riverdust that our ancestors once used mindpatterns as a weapon against each other. Even now, the war of mindpatterns is known as the Dread War, and the old ones speak of it in whispersmells. Long ago, we made an oath never to use the mindpattern weapon lightly. But it is also written in the Leafbox that a time will come when we will use the ancient weapon to save ourselves from a race of star creatures."

Maggie's face went suddenly cold and her hands clammy. "You mean . . . *we're* the star creatures? Peaches and Forest think the prophecy is coming true?"

Osmyrrah's odor of ammonia was pure and piercing as she regarded the children with bright, space-black eyes. "We must go to your city," she buzzed. "Let us show your people that we can be friends. Our danger is smaller than a speck of ash compared to the danger that will come to all if the mindpatterns are joined into a weapon."

"But the council will never believe us," said William. "Not unless we can *prove* how dangerous these . . . these mindpatterns are. Could you give them some kind of demonstration, Osmyrrah?"

The hint of a smell like cold, clean wind accompanied Osmyrrah's words as she said, "The mindpatterns of one person alone are not strong. We do not eat. We do not sleep. We lie in the water. *Waterdinner.* The water makes us strong. But even when I am in waterdinner, my mindpatterns alone are barely strong enough to move a bubble ship."

William shook his head frantically and raised a hand palm outward as if to stop the rush of unfamiliar words. "Wait a minute, wait a minute. You're going too fast. *Waterdinner? Bubble ships?*"

"Yeah. What's a bubble ship?" said Maggie.

Osmyrrah raised a tentacled leg toward the sky above the city, where several spider beasts rode through the air inside water-filled transparent spheres. "Those are bubble ships. We sometimes use them for fast travel, though they make us tired quickly."

"So *that's* what those things are. We've been wondering!" exclaimed William.

"Hey, we could have Osmyrrah take a bubble ship to New Genesis! It would prove that mindpatterns really exist at least," said Maggie.

"I'm not so sure," said William. "And besides, I

don't think that's what we want to do. That might just scare everybody even more. What we want to do is prove that *friendship* can really exist between us.''

A chaotic rush of smells flowed from Osmyrrah. Some were familiar—the smell of river reeds, lightning, and a sharp aroma like the bruised rind of a lemon. Others were new and indescribable. Maggie longed to know what they meant.

''Please, William. Maggie. We must go to your crater now. Perhaps it is not too late. Perhaps if they see us together as friends, the fear and anger of your people will disappear.''

William looked at Maggie questioningly. ''Shall we go?'' he said.

Maggie looked away, beyond the swift river, beyond the crystal city and the bluish grass of the meadows, to the point where the crater rim met the morning sky. She imagined a long line of colonists standing shoulder-to-shoulder on that rim, laser rifles at the ready. She shivered. ''Yeah. Let's go,'' she said.

The children had walked up and down the obsidian trail to the crystal cavern so many times that by now it felt quite familiar. They no longer tiptoed along with their arms out for balance on the glassy surface. Instead they stepped ahead with confidence, trusting their grip-sole boots. It took only a few minutes to reach the top.

But they had gone no more than a meter or two into the mouth of the cavern when a voice came out of the shadows in front of them. ''Well, here are our little friends!'' It was a *human* voice, a bit too hearty, and all too well known.

Ludlow Brak and Bilcher stepped out from behind a huge quartz boulder.

"What are you doing here?" cried Maggie.

"I might well ask you the same question, my dear," said Brak, grinning, his eyes shining from behind the narrowed slits of his thick, pink eyelids.

Osmyrrah faced Brak and Bilcher without a sound. She didn't need to say anything. Wave after wave of ozone cascaded from her.

CHAPTER EIGHT

Kidnapped

MAGGIE'S THROAT FELT SUDDENLY PARCHED, and her feet seemed to have grown roots that kept her from moving. She tried to look brave, but she could not stop herself from trembling, and she knew her face must be pale.

Brak slid his tongue around inside his cheek and smiled. He looked calm and confident. "We hope we're not interrupting anything," he said. "Ah, the troublesome Murdock children. I might have known I would find you here."

Beside him, Bilcher grinned vacantly as if he were only half listening. His silver tooth gleamed in the phosphorescent light.

William squared his shoulders and lifted his chin as he said, *"We* have a good reason for being here, Councilor Brak. We're trying to stop a war."

Brak chuckled. "Trying to stop a war? Single-handed? You arrogant, foolish child." He crossed his thick arms on his chest. He reminded Maggie of the stout wild cindercats that sometimes killed the colony's sheep. They would sink their teeth into an animal's hind leg and hang on until the quarry dropped from exhaustion.

"If anything," Brak continued, "you have *started* a war."

Maggie found her voice. Anger and indignation poured through her. "What do you mean?" she cried. "You're the one who wants the war. You're the one who made up that lie about being attacked. That's right! We *know* you're lying."

Brak clucked softly. "You're so unreasonable, my little friend. I'm a brave and peace-loving fellow, wouldn't you say? After all, I've come here to stop *you* from starting a war. The facts speak for themselves."

William knotted his hands into fists as he said, "You'd better explain right now what you mean by that."

"Just this, my boy. They've discovered that you're missing. And somehow, a rumor has started in the colony that you and your sister have been kidnapped by aliens. I'm sorry. Truly I am. I don't know how this mix-up happened. But I thought, since I'm the only other person who knows exactly where this crater is, it was my duty to come and investigate." Brak smiled.

Osmyrrah stood as if frozen. The ozone smell that had surrounded her like an electrical storm began to change until it resembled something more like iodine or melted copper. "You are not sorry. Why do you say something that is not the case?" she buzzed.

Surprise crossed Brak's face like the shadow of a

cloud. "How clever. You've taught the beast to say a few things."

"For your information, Councilor Brak, this 'beast' speaks Spacers Standard fairly well. She's understood everything that you've said," William replied.

Brak snorted and uncrossed his arms. "Oh, really? Well then why is it calling me a liar?"

"I know that you are not sorry," said Osmyrrah, stepping forward ever so slightly.

Bilcher nudged Brak and sneaked a glance along the tunnel toward the outside of the crater. "Luddy, let's go. They'll be waiting for us," he whispered.

But Maggie heard him clearly. "Who's waiting? What is this?"

Brak narrowed one green eye as he said, "I suggest that you come back to Mount Jackson with us and get this straightened out. Captain Stone is waiting outside in a ground sled, and as you can imagine, he's *very* anxious to see you in good health. It's up to you, of course. Just remember. If you refuse to come, and there's a war, it will be *your* fault."

"It doesn't matter, Brak," said Maggie. "We were on our way back anyway."

"Yes. Osmyrrah is coming, too. And for your information, we're going to prove once and for all that humans and spider beasts can be friends!" said William.

To the children's surprise, Brak smiled and said, "Fine, my boy. Nothing would please me more. You lead the way. We'll be right behind you." He held out his arm as if to invite them through a doorway. Beside him, Bilcher grinned broadly.

William glanced at Maggie and shrugged. "Okay," he said. "Let's go."

With a little shiver, she stepped after him. Something felt wrong. Her scalp prickled with the certainty that Brak was still up to no good. If only they had brought Starnight with them, she thought. If only William were brave enough to use it.

Osmyrrah walked beside the children as they continued through the tunnel toward the outside of the aliens' volcano. The smells of iodine and hot copper still poured from her, mixed now with smoky wariness and puzzlement.

They could see the faint peach-and-green glow of daylight sifting through the outside entrance to the cavern when Osmyrrah stopped abruptly and buzzed, "I wish to return to my city."

"But Osmyrrah!" cried Maggie. "You promised. You said you'd come back to Mount Jackson with us."

"I have changed my mind."

"But you can't!" Maggie was beside herself with disappointment. She shot a pleading look at William. But he stood motionless, a puzzled expression on his face.

Without even saying good-bye, Osmyrrah turned suddenly, pushed her way past Brak and Bilcher, and scuttled away through the cavern.

"Stop!" shouted Brak.

Bilcher raised his lightpistol and pulled the trigger. But Osmyrrah had already disappeared safely around a bend in the tunnel.

"Never mind," said Brak. "There'll be plenty of

time to teach the thing a lesson tomorrow. Now get along, children.'' He gave Maggie a little push.

She scowled at him, but walked on anyway, too stunned at Osmyrrah's apparent desertion and Brak's conceit to do anything else.

As the foursome walked through the mouth of the cavern, Maggie noticed that although Bilcher had replaced his lightpistol in its holster, he hadn't fastened the flap. Though she told herself she was being silly, her heart began to thud, and she couldn't help wondering which would be the best direction to run if they had to. She nudged William with her elbow, but he only frowned at her.

On the plain at the end of the tunnel sat two ground sleds. ''Aren't sleds a little extravagant for an errand like this?'' said William in a cutting tone.

''We're in a hurry,'' replied Bilcher and laughed. ''Right, Luddy?''

Maggie heard the small tearing sound of another holster flap being opened. By the time she turned to face Brak, he had a stun pistol in his hand. One of the sled hatches popped open, and Zerski emerged, also brandishing a pistol.

''How's Stone?'' said Brak.

''Out cold in the back passenger seat,'' answered Zerski, a broad smile splitting his jowly face. ''I don't think he'll be any problem. I gave him a little extra blast just for good measure.''

''Hey, what is this?'' cried William.

''A party, kid. What did you think?'' said Bilcher.

Maggie saw the broad, red stun ray flash from Bilcher's pistol, saw it light William's face for the briefest instant, saw William crumple to the ground. It took a moment before she really believed it had happened, and a moment more to overcome the horror that gripped her.

Bilcher stooped, threw William onto his shoulder as if he were a bundle of straw, and said, "Okay, Luddy. I'll take care of 'em now."

"See that you do, Bilcher. There's no room for mistakes," Brak replied.

Zerski climbed down from the sled hatch, and Bilcher disappeared through it, carrying William with him. Before Maggie could decide what to do, Zerski had a firm grip on her. The glass muzzle of his stun pistol felt cold and hard against her temple. "Don't move, dear," he said. "Luddy wants a word with you."

Maggie swallowed hard and watched the sled zoom away. In a moment, it was gone, leaving only a smooth swath in the sand.

Brak stood before her, looking fiercer and more cruel than she had ever seen him before. Maggie stared at his face, feeling almost as if she were someone else. Triumph had transformed his ruddy features into a laughing grimace that reminded her yet again of the cindercat.

"All my life, Maggie Murdock, people have laughed at me and treated me like a joke. Fiery little Ludlow Brak, full of big talk, too small to back his words up. Well, I'm through with that. We'll see what people think after Ludlow Brak has led the way to a better life for us all. By this time tomorrow, I'll be the leader of the richest colony on this planet—right here in your precious Osmyrrah's crater, where the soil and the weather are good enough to grow anything, and there's plenty of free labor in the form of spider beast slaves!''

"You're crazy, Brak. You think you can just walk in there and take their home away without a fight. Well, you're wrong!'' cried Maggie.

Brak grinned. She could almost smell the smugness that radiated from him. "Not crazy. No, no. Not crazy at all,'' he said through his smile. "They won't put up much of a fight. Not with the Watchers of Space on our side.''

Maggie's mouth felt dry as sand, and when she tried to speak, only a tiny croak came out.

"That's good, my little friend. I see you're in the mood to help me already.'' Brak reached down and grabbed Maggie by the collar of her coveralls. She whimpered in spite of herself as Zerski's pistol dug into her temple. "I want that sword of William's, and you are going to get it for me if you ever want to see your brother alive again.''

Those words of Brak's hurled Maggie out of control, sucked at her like a black hole in space. This one last injustice, heaped upon all the others, was more than she could bear. She screamed—a long, wild cry. "No-o-o-o-o!''

Perhaps she struggled without knowing it. Perhaps her scream alarmed Zerski into pulling the trigger. She never knew for sure. For an instant, the stun ray wrapped her in a shroud of pain. As she lay in the sand, with the last bits of consciousness crinkling out of her brain, she fancied that she saw a crystal sphere far off in the sky. *Osmyrrah,* she thought, before darkness overcame her. *Please let it be Osmyrrah.*

* * *

William opened his eyes and blinked to focus them. He could hardly believe what he saw. Far above him rose a domed, translucent ceiling so distant that at first he thought it was the sky. Hundreds of hollow crystal spheres hung suspended from it, like giant soap bubbles in a complex dance of peach-colored sunlight. He felt sweat trickling down his forehead. The air was very warm. He heard a roaring sound, muffled as if it came from far away or traveled through feathers before it reached his ears. He was lying on something hard—a floor of milky quartz.

Twisting, he tried to sit up. But as soon as he moved, he discovered that his hands were bound behind his back and his ankles were tied with sturdy ropes. He had to roll onto his side and hunch into a little ball in order to get himself upright. Slowly, details flowed back to him. Brak. Bilcher. The stun pistol. ''Maggie!'' he cried.

''Take it easy, William. She's not here. It's just you and I, I'm afraid. And dear old Bilcher, of course. He's gone off to get some water.'' The voice was a familiar one—kind, firm, and reassuring.

''Captain Stone,'' said William, groaning as he tested his ropes. They were so tight they hurt. ''Where are we? What happened?''

The captain shook his head. ''I don't know.'' The wrinkles in his forehead and around his kind, gray eyes were more prominent than William had ever seen them before. ''Bilcher isn't talking. But I'm sure Luddy Brak has something to do with this. I had a little chat with him about the danger of raising an army against an enemy we know nothing about. I also asked him some detailed questions about this spider beast who supposedly attacked him. His answers were so confused and contradictory that not even *he* could pretend to be telling the truth any longer. I'm afraid I lost my temper after that. I told him I intended to call another council meeting, and said I'd make him very sorry for having lied.''

The captain closed his eyes and laughed very softly. ''It was a stupid thing for me to do. Never back your enemy into a corner. That's what they say. When I got back to my cabin, somebody was waiting for me with a stun pistol. I don't know who. I never even got a look at him.''

William blinked away sweat and exhaled slowly. ''Yeah. It's Brak all right. Maggie and I . . . well . . . we sneaked out of New Genesis and went to warn the spider beasts about Brak's army after the council meeting. Osmyrrah told us that as far as she knows, none of her people have been killed, by Brak or anybody else. It *proves* Brak's lying about that attack story.''

''It just confirms what I was already convinced of,'' said the captain, shaking his head.

''Brak and Bilcher showed up just as we were leaving the alien crater. They told us there was a rumor in New Genesis that we'd been kidnapped by the spider beasts. Blast him! If there *is* such a rumor, he probably started it himself.'' Anger bubbled up inside William like a hot geyser. ''He told us if we didn't go back to Mount Jackson with him right away, there was going to be a war and it would be *our* fault. So we went with him, and as soon as we got out to the plain, they used a stun pistol on me. I don't know what he did with Maggie. Every word that comes out of Brak's mouth is a lie. And what for? Why is he doing all this? It seems so senseless!'' In frustration, William strained against his ropes until he winced with pain.

"Easy, now," said the captain. "It'll do you no good to hurt yourself."

"Maggie's right!" William cried. "I don't know why, but he *wants* us to be afraid of the spider beasts. He *wants* a war."

The captain closed his eyes and leaned back against his ropes. "Yes. He does want a war. He admitted his plan to me. He wants to take away the spider beasts' crater. He's convinced it's a richer, more fertile one than ours. He wants to establish a new colony there, with himself as leader. I guess you and I and Maggie just came too close to stopping him. Maybe that's why we're here, safely out of the way."

William licked his lips. They were parched and cracked, and the salt from his sweat made them sting. "But Brak doesn't know what he's getting into," he said. "If he thinks the spider beasts are just a bunch of docile animals, like a herd of sheep or something, he's dead wrong."

The captain raised his bushy gray eyebrows in a wordless question.

"They have a weapon. Something they call 'mind-patterns.' I don't know what it is exactly—some kind of mental force. It's so strange that Osmyrrah couldn't really explain it to us. And I'm afraid . . ." William's voice caught. "I'm afraid if Brak gets them mad enough, they'll use it. We'll *never* win a war against a weapon like that.''

"Mindpatterns!" said the captain. "Of course! Of course they could use it as a weapon!"

"You've heard of mindpatterns?"

"Yes, William, though I almost wish I hadn't. You see, the first translations of that alien book came out of the computer last night."

"The book!" cried William. "I'd forgotten about it. Did it explain mindpatterns?"

The captain nodded, hunching forward as if an invisible leaden necklace weighed him down. "As far as we can tell from what we read, the aliens have the ability to move things without touching them. They submerge themselves in geothermally heated water and ingest chemicals and minerals from it instead of eating. While they are submerged, and have access to that extra energy, they can move things. Just by thinking about it. Just by using what they call 'mindpatterns.' Imagine the things they could move by concentrating together. Cities. Armies. Nothing could stand in their way."

William looked up at the ceiling again, trying to breathe slowly and evenly, trying to get control of the fear that had suddenly grabbed him. Rays of light flowed like honey through the crystal roof. Sun glanced off the transparent spheres and danced in rainbow patterns on the quartz floor. He wished he knew where he was, but he could not even make a guess. Still more important, he wished he knew where Maggie was and what had happened to her.

He felt almost as desperate and helpless now as he had the time he'd fallen off the hull of the starship and been flung into space without a safety line. Brak had them where he wanted them, and he was strong. Maybe too strong to be stopped by anybody but the Watchers. Now there was something that frightened him even more than that.

William thought of the crystal spheres—ships without engines, powered only by mindpatterns. He looked up at the ceiling again, where fragile spheres hung like mammoth clusters of frogs' eggs. Alien bubble ships, like the ones he had seen flying through the air in Osmyrrah's crater—only empty. "I think I know where we are," he whispered.

"Where?"

"Smoky Top. The alien ruins at Smoky Top."

Captain Stone whistled softly. "Smoky Top? But that's an active volcano." A trickle of sweat ran down his cheek. "Heaven help us. If it is Smoky Top, we might find ourselves buried under fifty meters of hot lava any second."

Chapter Nine

Maggie and the Mudbaby

MAGGIE HEARD A NOISE LIKE THE ANGRY whirring of the fat New World bees in the orchards of Mount Jackson. The air smelled dusty, like soil and dried grain. She opened her eyes, expecting to see green sky or perhaps the metal ceiling of the Earth chamber aboard the starship Genesis. Instead she saw dark walls made of river reeds. Stripes of reddish afternoon sunlight crept in between the slender stalks. She felt as if she might still be dreaming. Where was she?

She fought her way through grogginess that clung to her like cobwebs. Finally, she sat up, only to be hit by a muddy swirl of dizziness so strong that it felt almost solid. Trembling, she lay back again and closed her eyes. Her hands and feet tingled as if from frostbite, and she ached all over. Dozens of questions rocketed through her mind as she began to remember what had happened. What had Brak done with William? Where was she?

As she lay in the cool darkness, she realized with a start that the noise she had heard was not the buzz of New World bees after all. It was the sound of a crowd. Above that windy muttering, the voice of Ludlow Brak stretched like a thin wire.

"My friends, whatever we do, we must act together—with unity. Two children, and now Captain Stone as well, have been kidnapped by the aliens. We can no longer stand by, looking defenseless, waiting for them to make some larger move. We must take the initiative now! Before it's too late! We must rescue our people. We must attack!"

Maggie groaned and sat up again. "Brak, you liar!" She wanted to shout it, but her tongue felt like a lump of rubber, and her voice was only a faint squeak.

She looked around in the dim light. She seemed to be inside a storage shed of some kind. Field tools rested in haphazard confusion against the walls. Some of them had broken handles or prongs, some were rusty and bent. All of them were caked with dried, greenish mud. Bulging sacks of grain, compost, and manure lay at random on the floor. By poking her finger through a hole in the cloth, she discovered that she was sitting on a bag of river nut seeds.

Maggie wobbled to her feet. Brushing off her hands, she surveyed the shed. There were no windows. She crept over to the door and gave it a strong, steady push, but it didn't budge. As noiselessly as she could, she made her way over to one of the walls and peered through a slit between two reeds.

What she saw made her feel empty inside. A huge crowd of people milled about on the New Genesis town square. Ludlow Brak stood before them on a raised platform, his brow furrowed, his arms spread wide. His usually immaculate white coat looked a little rumpled, and his collar hung open, giving him the air of a hard-working man who has not had enough sleep.

"We must raise an army," he was shouting. "We must free the captives, and show the aliens our mettle. We must keep our pride as human beings intact." A growing roar issued from the crowd like the sound of an earthquake.

She heard someone cry, "I volunteer! They've got my son and my daughter, and I want them back!"

Sickness wrenched Maggie's stomach as she recognized the voice of her own father. "No, Dad! He's lying . . . can't you see?" she cried. But her shouts disappeared like whispers in the storm of the angry gathering. No, she thought. Of course he can't see. Brak's too good at this game.

She was on the verge of throwing herself against the wall, trying to break out, when she heard a tiny scratching noise at the door. She turned, suddenly afraid in the dim reddish light.

"Who is it?" she called. Her voice sounded small and hollow. There was no answer. Only the rattle of metal against metal. The door swung slowly outward. Maggie shrank into a dark corner. Her fingers curled around the handle of an old rake. Fresh air wafted into the shed, carrying with it the rank smells of the fertile fields and the scent of something else: roses, and clean water.

"Osmyrrah?" Maggie whispered, picking up the rake.

She heard a rattling buzz. "Maggie."

Maggie took a huge breath and exhaled loudly as Osmyrrah appeared in the doorway, framed in afternoon sunlight, a peculiar-looking tool clutched in her tentacles.

"Maggie, we must get away from here."

"How did you find me? How did you get the door open?" said Maggie, stepping across the seed bags with her arms out for balance.

"I opened the door with this." Osmyrrah waved the small, transparent tool, then placed it in her leaf bag. "I watched from a bubble ship. I saw everything. They have taken William to the Mountain of the Dead. We must help him. Please. We must go. They will find us here."

"Where did you say they took William and the captain?" Maggie asked.

But Osmyrrah did not seem to hear. "I can run fast," she buzzed. "You could sit on my back."

"Sure . . . sure. Whatever you say," said Maggie. She climbed onto Osmyrrah's carapace, straddling the beautiful crystal disk set into her sleek fur. Osmyrrah reached around and steadied her with a set of warm tentacles.

"Are you ready?" she buzzed.

"I think so, but we'd better go to my cabin before we do anything else. There's something there that Brak wants—William's sword. He's never going to get his dirty hands on Starnight. I'm taking it with us to William. The Watchers are our only chance of stopping a war now."

"Which way is your cabin?"

"That way." Maggie pointed. "If we stay off the road and stick to the wheat fields, maybe nobody will see us."

"I am afraid," said Osmyrrah. "What if Brak finds us?"

Maggie squeezed Osmyrrah with all her might. "I'm afraid, too. But I guess we just have to take the chance. There's no other way."

Faster than a Jubilation River hare, more swiftly than a crystal lacewing, Osmyrrah darted through the doorway and out into the orange light of day without making a sound. In the near distance, Maggie heard Brak shouting and the crowd cheering again.

"Please don't let him see us!" she prayed as Osmyrrah carried her at desperate speed across the roadway and into the tall grass beyond.

Maggie pressed herself tight against Osmyrrah's back and closed her eyes to keep out the dust that flew from the tall wheat as they passed. Sharp stems and bristly clusters of kernels scratched her cheeks and hands, but she dared not cry out. The noise of the crowd on the square grew fainter and fainter until at last Osmyrrah stopped.

"I must rest," she buzzed softly.

With her ear pressed against the spider beast's carapace, Maggie thought she heard the ebb and flow of Osmyrrah's blood in a rhythm much faster than seemed right. She glanced back in the direction from which they had come. Osmyrrah had left a wide swath of bent wheat. Her body was exactly the wrong shape for traveling through tall grass, and Maggie could see why the effort had tired her.

"I could go faster on the road," said Osmyrrah.
"Do you think it is safe now?"

Maggie peered through the wheat. The road lay deserted in the reddening dusk. "I don't know . . . if we stay in the wheat we'll leave a trail all the way to the cabin. They'll find us for sure. The road's risky, but almost everybody in the colony is in that crowd on the town square. We might get away with it."

She looked back once more, then patted Osmyrrah and said, "Okay. Let's take the road. Whenever you're ready."

The wheat bent and rustled as Osmyrrah made her way out of the field. As soon as she reached the hard, greenish gray surface of the road, she raced away at an incredible pace. The fields, houses, and orchards they passed became little more than a blur. Afraid of falling, Maggie clung so tightly to Osmyrrah's back that her fingers ached.

Luck was with them. In their headlong rush for the Murdock cabin, the two fugitives passed only one person. Old Louie Etcheberry, who paid little attention to politics, happened to be herding a small flock of his prize speckled sheep to a new pasture instead of cheering for Brak in the town square. Louie did not seem the least bit surprised at the sight of Osmyrrah. In fact, he smiled and waved as they rushed past. He leaned on his staff while his dog, Pancho, barked and yapped to keep the skittish sheep from running away. Maggie's heart thundered in her ears as she wondered whether Louie would tell anyone that he had seen them. She crossed her fingers and hoped he would for-

get about it, at least until his sheep had arrived safely in
their new pasture.

Because Maggie's parents were both at the town
square, the cabin was empty when she and Osmyrrah
arrived. Osmyrrah, too large to move freely in the narrow hallway, stood just inside the front door while
Maggie raced into William's room. She ran to the
closet and released the spring latch of the secret compartment. There lay Starnight, in an undulating pool of
orange light. Just looking at it made Maggie feel fierce
and joyful, and very much stronger than Brak.

She slung the sword in its sheath over her shoulder.
Like a miniature copperdust storm, she rushed through
the cabin, stuffing her beltpack and pockets with fresh
supplies of food, water canisters, and survival gear.

"Okay, Osmyrrah. Let's go get William," she said.

But Osmyrrah did not move. She was trembling.
"Maggie, I must go to the river."

"What's the matter?" said Maggie. Her stomach
felt as if gravity had suddenly disappeared. "Are you
feeling okay?"

"I must lie in the water until two moons rise. Is there
. . . a quiet place in the river? Where no one will find
me?" The words were so blurry that Maggie could
hardly make them out. Osmyrrah was producing a
strange mineral smell, like the stench that rose from the
geysers and boiling mud pots along the river. Her
brown fur, which usually lay flat and shining against
her carapace, now stood upright like freshly cut grass.

Maggie tugged at her dusty hair, barely able to
think. From New Genesis northward, both shores of
the Jubilation River bustled with activity. Cultivated

fields and orchards came nearly to the banks. There were bridges and boat landings, irrigation stations and hydroelectric boosters every few meters. No chance for privacy there.

A little more than a kilometer south of town, though, the soil became thin and rocky, and the spaces between fields grew wider. The colonists paid little attention to the short stretch of river between the southernmost bridge and the crater wall. The west bank was virtually deserted. The east bank was a rocky wilderness of mud pots and sulfur pools. No plants except the hearty, native scarlet-reeds would grow there, and the stench of sulfur made it less than pleasant even for bathing. Moreover, large reptilian creatures called mudbabies inhabited some of the cooler mud pots. They emerged frequently to catch and eat small river creatures, and they had been known to attack colonists now and then. Maggie had never been able to forget the time big Jim Rassmussen the geologist had his hand and arm nearly shredded by a mudbaby's small, razorlike teeth. She shivered and wondered which would be worse— dealing with Brak or fighting off a mudbaby. It didn't take long to decide.

"I know a place on the river where nobody will bother us," she said. "It's a couple of kilometers south of here. Do you think you can make it?"

"How far is a couple of kilometers?" said Osmyr-rah.

Maggie thought for a moment. "Well, it's about the distance between the crystal arch and the foot of the obsidian trail in your crater."

"I can go that far, and I can carry you."

"Are you sure? I could walk. Maybe that would be better."

"No. Too slow. I need the river before dark."

"Okay," said Maggie, "but you have to promise to tell me if you get too tired."

Osmyrrah said nothing.

Maggie sighed. "We'd better get moving before somebody catches us here." She stuck her head out the door and looked up and down the road. Still deserted. "Let's go," she said.

Osmyrrah scuttled through the doorway. Maggie climbed onto her back, and they raced away to the south.

The shadow of the crater's west wall advanced steadily toward the road like the vanguard of a dark army as Maggie and Osmyrrah sped along. By the time they reached the south bridge, the river lay in twilight. As the air grew cooler, swirling white mist gathered above the warm water. The foul smell of decayed reeds and sulfur floated up to them along with the eerie night cries of the creatures that lived in the volcanic marshes. Maggie shuddered, afraid of what waited for them in the oozing mud pots below, wondering about Osmyrrah's urgent need for the river. It had to have something to do with waterdinner. How long would they be delayed? For her own part, Osmyrrah carried them over the bridge and down the east bank without the least sign of hesitation. She might have been walking eagerly along a sunny avenue, for all the fear she showed.

"Will anyone find us here?" Osmyrrah asked, stopping at last in a stand of scarlet-reeds. Nearby lay a deep, quiet pool, protected from the swift current by a natural levee of boulders.

Maggie dismounted and stood on tiptoes, peering across the river. She could hardly see the road; the boulders and fuzzy-topped reeds made an excellent hiding place. "Nobody ever goes south of the bridge. And if they did, they'd never be able to see us from the road. I think we're safe."

Osmyrrah slid the leaf bag over her mandibles and laid it on a dry rock caked with yellow crystals. "Maggie, do you remember waterdinner? I must lie in the water. The water makes me strong. Waterdinner. Do you understand?"

Maggie nodded, though she wished she understood more completely; she felt ignorant and afraid.

"Will you be asleep?" she asked timidly. "Will I be alone very long?"

"Remember, Maggie? I do not sleep. I do not eat. Waterdinner. I am sorry. I must lie in the water until two moons rise."

"It's . . . it's okay," said Maggie, unable to stop her voice from shaking a little.

"Will you wait for me?" said Osmyrrah as she backed toward the river.

"I'll wait! Don't worry—I'll wait! Good-bye!" But Osmyrrah had already disappeared into the murky pool, leaving only an eddy in the patchy mist.

Maggie walked to the water's edge, leaned down, and waved the vapor away as well as she could. Just for an instant, she thought she saw the round shape of Osmyrrah's carapace lying just below the dark surface.

Then the mist closed in again and she was left alone, staring at nothing.

Uneasily, she looked up at the greenish black sky, where the first stars were already appearing. Somewhere behind her she heard the steady *glug-glug* of a boiling mud pot. The mournful call of a three-winged wailer made a shiver run up her spine. She had never heard of a wailer's attacking a human being, but in the darkness anything seemed possible.

Maggie felt suddenly very glad for Starnight's faint warmth against her side. She patted the sword's hilt. Taking out her pocket torch, she shone it among the reeds. The slim beam revealed a dry slab of volcanic rock near the riverbank. She reached into one of her thigh pockets and took out a small piece of silvery cloth, then opened it up into a full-sized blanket, thin but warm. Wrapping it around her, she climbed up onto the rock to wait.

She could barely smell the malodorous mud pots anymore, and the distant rush of the warm river soothed her like a lullaby. She was very tired. She knew that it was well past suppertime and that she ought to be hungry as well. But her stomach felt light and jittery, as if she had been in zero-gravity all day. She satisfied herself with a few sips of water from one of her canisters.

Maggie put her hands behind her head and lay back on the hard rock, her mind racing. By now, Brak had probably discovered that she had escaped from the storage shed. She smiled, imagining the look on his face when he found the door gaping wide and the shed empty. Then she remembered the threat he had made as

Zerski held the stun pistol to her head. *I want that sword of William's, and you are going to get it for me if you ever want to see your brother alive again.* She wished she had heard what Osmyrrah had said—the name of the place where they had taken William and the captain. Her smile flickered out like a tiny flame in the wind, and she wished desperately that Osmyrrah had not insisted on coming to the river. Time was passing, and time was something that neither she and Osmyrrah nor Brak's captives could afford to waste.

Yet she couldn't blame Osmyrrah. She remembered how the spider beast had trembled, how the fur had stood up on her back. Osmyrrah knew that every minute was critical if they were to succeed in rescuing William and Captain Stone. Maggie felt certain that something awful would have happened if Osmyrrah had not gotten to the river for waterdinner in time. But what? She wished that she could dive into the misty pool, pull Osmyrrah to the surface, and ask her all the questions that now ran through her mind like mad judabuckles. But the answers would have to wait . . . until two moons had risen, at least.

Maggie gazed up at the stars, beginning to feel drowsy and warm. She had always had trouble keeping track of the moons. Even William had to use a calculator to tell which of the three moons would be visible at what times, how much of each moon would lie in shadow and how much in light. Maggie's own knowledge of lunar activities was sketchy at best. Two of the moons were small and reddish. She always had trouble telling them apart. The third moon was easy, because it was very large and shone with a bright golden light.

But she saw no moons at all tonight, at least not yet. The stars seemed very clear—little lights, big lights, like a distant town in a huge, dark valley.

All at once, Maggie heard a low, growling hiss. At the same time she felt something warm and slimy on her cheek. Her nostrils burned with the horrible reek of sulfur.

With a shriek, Maggie rolled off the rock, clutching with both hands at the thing on her face. Jerking and twisting, she pulled off what felt like a muddy, writhing snake. A searing pain ran up the side of her face as she flung the creature away, barely noticing how heavy it was. Shaking mud from her eyes, she leaped to her feet. Facing her, poised for a fresh attack, was a meter-long mudbaby, its sharp teeth glittering in the starlight!

CHAPTER TEN

The Mountain of the Dead

MAGGIE GRABBED STARNIGHT'S HILT AND tried to yank the sword from its sheath. The mudbaby crouched on its six stubby legs, switching its snaky tail back and forth, glaring at her with small, wet eyes. She tugged again at the sword, but her hands were slick with sweat and mud, and the sheath fit too tightly. Her face felt as if it were on fire.

The creature snarled at her. Dripping with gray ooze from its mud pot den, it looked like something dragged from a grave, something that shouldn't be alive at all. Maggie's breath tore from her throat in ragged whimpers, too fast, too fast, as the mudbaby hissed and opened its mouth. Rings of tiny, dully gleaming teeth marched all the way down its gullet. A ghastly memory flashed through her mind, of big Jim Rassmussen running down the road to the infirmary, his shirt in shreds and his arm dripping blood. That was all it took. With both hands, Maggie wrenched Starnight free of its

132

sheath and heaved it point-first at the hideous creature. The mudbaby squealed, turned, and skittered away into the reeds.

Starnight stood upright, quivering with the force of Maggie's thrust, its tip stuck firmly in the crack between two chunks of pitchstone. A pool of magical orange radiance shivered on the rocks around it. Maggie held still, too dazed and breathless to move. She could almost feel the power of the sword, in her tingling fingertips, in the blaze of sudden warmth across her shoulders. Her legs shook. The river and the reeds seemed to spin slowly around her as she reached up and touched her cheek. Her fingers came away covered with mud and blood. The burning sensation had spread along her jawbone and down her neck. She felt as if she'd been stung by a giant New World bee.

When her breath had slowed and her knees seemed a little stronger, Maggie stumbled into the pool of light, grabbed Starnight's hilt, and pulled the sword out of the crack. A bit of the mudbaby's scaly skin clung to the glowing blade, and she smiled triumphantly, pretending that it was skill and not luck that had guided Starnight to its mark.

"So there, you stinking mudbaby!" she cried into the dark reeds. "That'll teach you to pick a fight with Maggie Murdock!"

She hefted the sword, relishing its balance and solid weight. Just holding it made her feel better. She wondered if this was how William felt after he had killed the Unhappy One. Maggie bit her lip, remembering how William had returned to the Genesis sad, weak, and injured, how he had wanted only to sleep and be left alone. No. There was more to being heroic than just scaring off a mudbaby with a big sword.

Maggie walked shakily to the riverbank, lay down on her stomach, and splashed her face with warm water. She suspected that the sulfurous mud made her cheek sting, so she washed the scratch thoroughly with a piece of disinfectant soap from her survival kit. When she was finished she sat down to rest on a rock beside the quiet pool into which Osmyrrah had disappeared. She laid Starnight across her knees and stared into the swirling mist for a long time, but no movement disturbed the water, and no moons rose in the dark sky. After a while, her head nodded forward. Startled, she realized that she must have dozed off. Her joints felt stiff with chill and inactivity, and her cheek burned worse than ever. All she wanted was to climb into a warm bed and go to sleep.

But there was no warm bed unless she made one for herself. Maggie got up, struggling with arms and legs that felt heavy as bricks. Swinging Starnight like a sickle, she cut the fluffy tops off some of the river reeds. These she gathered into her blanket and transported to the flat slab of rock, where she fashioned them into a makeshift mattress. Several heated stones from the edge of a small geyser vent provided the last touch of luxury to her new bed. She could hardly keep her eyes open as she climbed into the pile of soft, warm fuzz and covered herself with the blanket. With her fingers wrapped tightly around Starnight's hilt, she fell asleep, drifting into a long dream in which she joined Osmyrrah in the silent depths of a warm, watery darkness.

* * *

Maggie awoke slowly, rising through layers of sleep as if she were climbing stairs. She had the feeling that she must be sitting up. But that was impossible, because she was looking straight into the sky, where two moons hung like gold and copper coins. The river rushed as it plunged over stones, the mud pots chugged and gurgled, a breeze sang in the reeds. Her forehead felt very cold, and her cheeks felt very hot.

Two moons! She threw off her blanket, grabbed Starnight's hilt, and sat up, dangling her legs over the side of her rocky bed. For a moment, she wasn't sure she could get to her feet. Blood pounded painfully in her temples, and she shivered with a sudden chill. She wished she had a mirror, because the left side of her face felt as if it were puffed up like a Jubilation mushroom. But there were two moons in the sky, and Osmyrrah had said she'd be back when two moons had risen. There was no way to even guess what terrible things might be happening to Brak's captives this moment. There was no way to guess how much longer it would take Brak to force New Genesis into a fatal war with the spider beasts. There wasn't an instant to be wasted.

She plunged Starnight into the muddy ground and used it as a staff to help her stand up. Walking turned out to be a separate problem all by itself. She had trouble making her legs work right, for they felt almost as if they belonged to someone else. A nagging fear grew steadily within her. Simple fatigue did not seem to account entirely for her troubles. The scratch on her cheek had come from the mudbaby, she was certain, though she couldn't say whether teeth or claws had done the damage. She had never heard of a poisonous mudbaby before, but that didn't mean much. Almost every day the colonists discovered creatures they had never seen or heard of before. Maggie shivered again and tried not to think about it. Perhaps it was just the aftereffects of Zerski's stun pistol that made her feel so ill.

When she got to the river, there was still no sign of Osmyrrah. Maggie touched her sore cheek gingerly and muttered, "Blast it, Osmyrrah, where are you? You promised. The moons are up, and you promised."

Clinging to Starnight's glowing hilt, she looked up at the stars, then back down at the pool and the steamy mist that rose from it. She cupped her hands to her mouth and called, "Osmyrrah!"

No answer. She called again, but neither the mist nor the water moved. Maggie leaned over and tried to wave the mist away as she had done when Osmyrrah first entered the pool. But her pocket torch was too weak to illuminate more than the top few centimeters of water. She bent and picked up a rock about the size of her fist. She tossed it into the pool, then picked up several more and tossed them in, too.

"Hey!" she shouted. "Come out of there. We have to get going! The moons are up."

When the spider beast did not appear, Maggie stamped her foot and hobbled off to get more rocks. She felt anger growing like an ascending weather balloon inside her. Just how long could waterdinner take? Osmyrrah must be having a regular banquet down there! If the spider beast didn't come soon, Maggie decided, she wasn't going to waste any more time waiting. She would blasted well find William without Osmyrrah.

But even as she formulated these brave thoughts, she had to stop and wipe sweat from her forehead, first puffing then shivering as sudden waves of hot and cold washed over her.

"I'm not sick," she cried aloud. "I refuse to be sick!" She slipped on a treacherous stone, fell to her knees in the mud, and tried hard to keep from crying. "I won't, I won't!" she whispered. "I won't be sick and I won't cry."

Suddenly she heard the gush of water as something large emerged from the pool. Not quite able to get to her feet, she twisted around for a better look. There stood Osmyrrah, her wet fur dripping and steaming in the cool night air, the fragrance of roses and rain pouring from her, the sweetest perfume Maggie could imagine.

"I am sorry. I tried to hurry," said Osmyrrah in a watery, burbling buzz.

"Oh, Osmyrrah!" Suddenly Maggie was laughing and crying both at the same time. "Oh, I'm so glad to see you."

Hurriedly she brushed away the tears and staggered up, anxious to prove that she was strong and well rested, frightened at the chance of being taken to the New Genesis infirmary instead of rescuing William. Maggie felt certain that whatever was wrong with her would go away soon. It *had* to.

Nevertheless, she wobbled as she got to her feet, and Osmyrrah had to steady her.

"What is wrong, Maggie?" she asked, clicking her mandibles.

Maggie gulped, smiled, and tried to look surprised. "Nothing's wrong. Why should anything be wrong?"

"That does not make sense." Osmyrrah backed away slightly. "Many things could be wrong." A complex mixture of smells drifted up from her, among them the tang of lightning and the burning-leaf pungency of curiosity.

"Your smell is different," said Osmyrrah. "What is wrong?"

Maggie blinked as an uncomfortable realization rushed in upon her. Maybe Osmyrrah could smell pain and fear. Maybe that was how she could tell that Brak had been lying when he intercepted them in the crystal tunnel. A spider beast's sense of smell had to be keen, for communication purposes if nothing else. Maggie knew that human beings had a lot of different smells. Her father smelled of cloves in the morning, and of sweat and machines when he came home after work. Her mother smelled of sweat, too, and of warm, damp earth when the fields were planted, of grain or roots or leaves when they were harvested. William smelled of the bluemint sprigs he loved to chew.

And what about Maggie? She pressed her lips together and leaned on Starnight to keep from trembling. She didn't smell like anything important or special. She probably smelled like schoolwork, or like the strong, homemade soap she used on her face and hands every morning. Right now she probably smelled more important than she ever had before in her life—like sulfur and mudbabies. And Osmyrrah thought it was all wrong.

"Nothing's wrong with the way I smell," she snapped. "I'm covered with this stinking mud, that's all."

Osmyrrah reached up and touched Maggie's cheek gently near the scratch the mudbaby had left. Maggie jerked away as if the soft tentacles were red hot.

"I do not understand," said Osmyrrah. "I see that something is wrong, yet you say there is nothing. How did this hurt come to you?"

"It's nothing. A mudbaby scratched me."

"What is a mudbaby?"

"Just one of those big lizards that lives in the mud pots," said Maggie, trying her hardest to feel irritated and not at all frightened. "Come on, Osmyrrah. We're wasting time. We've got to get to William. We've got to save him, and stop Brak from starting a war."

Osmyrrah did not have to speak as she retrieved her leaf bag from the dry rock where she had left it during waterdinner. She produced an eloquent array of scents—ozone richened by the sweet spiciness that Maggie associated with reassurance. Maggie could tell from the ozone that Osmyrrah was upset; from the other scents she could tell that Osmyrrah didn't want her to worry.

Maggie forced a laugh. "I'm not worried," she said. "Why should I worry?"

Osmyrrah took something that looked like a small, flat pebble from her bag. The pebble turned out to be soft and crumbly; either that or Osmyrrah's tentacle-fingers were stronger than Maggie had thought. The spider beast ground the pebble to powder, then added river water to make a thick paste.

"I will put this on your cheek," she said, reaching toward Maggie. "Maybe it will help."

Maggie closed her eyes, expecting pain when Osmyrrah smeared the paste on the scratch. To her surprise, it hurt very little—no more than the disinfectant swabs her mother used when Maggie skinned her knee or her elbow.

"I do not know what will happen," said Osmyrrah. "These creatures—you call them mudbabies?—some of them have stinging water on their teeth. It hurts a little, to make us go away. But you are so different from us. I think it hurts you more. I do not know."

Maggie touched her cheek carefully. It already seemed to feel better. "I'll be fine," she said. With both hands she replaced Starnight in its sheath. She looked into one of the spider beast's three eyes. "Osmyrrah, we've got to get to William. We can't wait any longer. Please. Please! Is it far?"

"Maggie, are you certain? I could take you home."

Maggie shook her head. "You know I can't go home. If Brak catches me, I'll probably end up stranded with William and the captain myself. What good would that do?" She forced a laugh. "You'd have to rescue all of us, and stop Brak's war by yourself. No. I can't risk going home. And besides, if anything happened to William . . ." She couldn't bear to finish the sentence.

The musty spiciness of reassurance drifted up from Osmyrrah again as she said simply, "I will carry you. It is not far. My bubble ship is waiting outside your crater."

Maggie clambered onto Osmyrrah's back, a little

clumsily but without help. She really did feel some-what better. Her limbs seemed more cooperative than they had a moment before, and her cheek felt less swol-len. As she clung to Osmyrrah's fur, she crossed her fingers and silently hoped that the spider beast's salve would soon cure her completely. The task that lay ahead promised to be difficult enough even for some-one who felt completely well and confident.

Osmyrrah sped west along the base of the crater wall, picking her way across the pitchstone and obsid-ian talus as if she had traveled it every day of her life. The light of the moons seemed to be more than enough for her three eyes. In no time at all the two travelers reached the foot of the crater-wall stairs. Osmyrrah climbed them swiftly and smoothly, just as lights be-gan to blink on in New Genesis for the late-night wake period. It was an odd time for any colonist to be abroad, and they passed no one as they hurried up the stairway, keeping to the shadows.

Once on the rim, Osmyrrah left the ashen trail and plunged down the side of the mountain toward the broad plain. When they reached the base of Mount Jackson, she scuttled abruptly into a hidden cleft formed by three giant crystals. There, in the quiet shel-ter of sand and crystal, stood a water-filled transparent sphere.

Maggie climbed down from Osmyrrah's back and nearly toppled into the sand. Her knees felt as if they needed oiling. She stared at the bubble ship, knowing that she might cry and too tired to fight it.

"Osmyrrah, I can't travel in a ship filled with water. I don't think this is going to work."

"It will work," said Osmyrrah, sending out a wave of fragrant spiciness. She indicated a large nodule on the side of the sphere. "It is small, but you can ride in this chamber, the water lock. Is that the word? I will give you air spheres. It is a short trip. All will be well."

Osmyrrah reached into her leaf bag and handed Maggie three small glass bubbles that looked empty. "If the air becomes foul, break one of these. It will help."

Maggie felt a chill of apprehension as she looked inside. No controls, no machinery, not even a chair to sit on. There was nothing inside the bubble ship except water, and nothing inside the water lock except air. "Are you sure this'll work?" she asked.

"It will work. Waterdinner powers it. And mindpatterns."

Maggie squinted across the plain, where moonlight sparkled on the faces of the giant crystals. "Where are we going?" she asked.

"To the Mountain of the Dead," said Osmyrrah, producing a smell that made the hair on the back of Maggie's neck slowly stand upright—the barest whiff of something ancient and terribly, terribly cold.

"What's the Mountain of the Dead?" Maggie's voice was hardly a whisper.

"Long ago, it was a city like our own. My nestparent and waterparent . . . they know the legend. They have studied the mountain and the Leafbox of Riverdust all their lives, though some say it is forbidden. All those in the city died because of the Dread War. They died from the mindpattern weapon. Since then, to show our sorrow, we place our dead there."

Maggie leaned close to Osmyrrah's comforting warmth as she thought of the Smoky Top expedition's report. *A vast open grave containing the corpses of thousands of huge spider or crablike creatures.* She shivered, perhaps from the mudbaby bite, perhaps from fear. It suddenly occurred to her that Brak could have gotten as many spider beast mandibles and as much carapace hair as he wanted from the corpses at Smoky Top. She felt so disgusted that she wanted to spit.

She pointed toward the faint plume of steam that marked Smoky Top far in the distance. "Is that the Mountain of the Dead, over there?"

"Yes," said Osmyrrah.

Maggie shut her eyes and tried to swallow back the dizziness that kept sweeping over her like wind in a wheat field. So it was true. Smoky Top and the Mountain of the Dead were one and the same place. Brak was holding William and Captain Stone in a place where no colonist would ever stumble across them by accident—a seething volcano where eruption was a possibility from each moment to the next.

"Let's hurry, Osmyrrah. Oh, please, let's hurry," she whispered.

Osmyrrah answered only with ozone and spice.

CHAPTER ELEVEN

Nestlings

MAGGIE STOOD BEFORE THE MOONLIT BUB-
ble ship, swaying, clutching Starnight's hilt. No stupid
mudbaby bite is going to stop me from helping William, she thought. She repeated it over and over to herself as she waited for her knees to stop shaking. Dimly,
she felt Osmyrrah's tentacles around her arm, steady-
ing her, helping her to stay on her feet.

Faint but undeniable, the smell of lightning hung in
the air, overpowering the rich scent of reassurance as
Osmyrrah said, "I am afraid, Maggie. You are sick. I
must take you home. There is too much danger for
you."

"No! No!" Maggie cried, blinking, trying with all
her might to overcome the milky fog that hung before
her eyes. "I'm fine. Come on. Let's get in the ship and
go."

The smoky scent of burning leaves replaced the
smell of ozone as Osmyrrah clicked her mandibles.

144

Recognizing the spider beast's message of perplexity and suspicion, Maggie said, "Look. I *promise*. I'm okay. Please, *please* take me to the Mountain of the Dead."

"No," said Osmyrrah. "Not until your smells match your words."

Maggie gritted her teeth and blinked back tears of pain and frustration. Osmyrrah knew she was lying, just as she had known that Brak was lying when he kidnapped William and Maggie from the cavern. At last Maggie admitted to herself that there was no way to deceive Osmyrrah. She could tell how a person felt about what they were saying just from the way they smelled.

"Osmyrrah, look, I . . . I'm sorry," Maggie stammered. "Don't you see how important this is? If we don't get Starnight to William as fast as we can . . . if we can't get the Watchers to help us stop Brak . . . don't you see? It doesn't matter how I feel. I've *got* to get to William and Captain Stone."

Osmyrrah stood in silence as a faint breeze moaned across the pinnacles of the giant crystals. "What if you die?" she said at last.

Maggie dug her fingernails into her palms, trying to distract herself from the terrifying sound of those words. For Osmyrrah had hit on the very fear that had haunted her ever since the mudbaby's attack. "I . . . I won't die," she said, her voice as thin as the light from a very small star.

"You might," said Osmyrrah.

Maggie closed her eyes as she thought once more of William, and of how empty the world would seem without him. "It doesn't matter," she said softly. "It doesn't matter, as long as I get Starnight to William before it happens.''

Osmyrrah contemplated her for a moment, looking for all the world like a milky stone statue in the shadow of the crystals. As if magic had turned stone to flesh, she bent her legs and slowly lowered herself until her heavy, ridged breast touched the sand. Then she raised herself again, all the while producing a smell that made Maggie feel as if she'd been plunged into a dream of long-forgotten places. It was a smell like vanilla, or freshly ground flour, mingled with a cold, clean scent like clouds.

Maggie watched in wonder, half-dazed, wordless.

When the strange ritual was over, Osmyrrah said, ''When I am older, and the season of dust comes, perhaps I will choose a mate, and tend our young ones in my nest. Then will I hope that my young possess mind-patterns as honorable as yours.'' Once again, Osmyrrah bent till she touched the sand. ''I believe that I understand you. I believe that I see now. From this time forward, may we be like young from the same nest. I am honored by you, nestling.''

Maggie tried to speak but couldn't. Relief, pride, and most of all, *joy* filled her too full. The dusty tears that escaped from her eyes had to speak for her.

Osmyrrah moved toward the bubble ship. ''We will go quickly,'' she said.

If Osmyrrah touched the transparent surface, Maggie did not see her do it. Nevertheless, an opening appeared in the large nodule on the side of the ship. Osmyrrah scuttled into it. ''I will go in first,'' she buzzed. ''When I am in the water, I will open the outer entrance again, and you must climb inside. Are you well enough to climb?''

"I think so,'' Maggie replied as she looked up at the opening. It was about a meter above the ground.

"Good,'' said Osmyrrah. As quickly as it had come, the opening disappeared. Once again, the nodule looked smooth and featureless. As Maggie watched, water flowed into the nodule. When it was full, Osmyrrah swam into the main compartment of the bubble ship. Immediately, the water began to disappear from the water lock again, leaving it dry and empty. Once more, the nodule opened up, this time to receive Maggie.

Maggie spat on her hands, grabbed the smooth edge of the hatchway, and scrambled up. The mudbaby venom made her feel so weak and tired that she almost couldn't manage. But thinking of William, she gave a mighty push and hooked one of her knees over the ledge. From there, it was fairly easy to pull herself into the water lock. Slumped panting against the clear wall, Maggie smiled and gave Osmyrrah the spacer's thumbs-up signal. The spider beast, floating freely in murky, mineral-filled water, watched Maggie through the glassy wall of the neighboring compartment. When Maggie glanced back at the outside, the opening in the water lock was gone again. The first part of Osmyrrah's plan had succeeded. The spider beast was sealed into the watery main compartment, while Maggie rode like precious baggage in the water lock.

All at once, Maggie became aware of motion. The bubble ship began to rise steadily upward. She clutched her stomach as she looked through the clear floor. Below, the gleaming crystals of the plain, the ashen trail, and the slopes of Mount Jackson dropped away with terrifying speed. Like a projectile hurled from a starship's jettison chute, the bubble ship flew into the sky.

Acceleration pressed Maggie against the curved wall of the water lock. She felt like an insect trapped between two pieces of glass. The moons of Earth II hung above the eastern horizon, shining jewels in a belt of frosty light that faded from rose and white-gold to green-black at the sky's zenith.

Her heart scurried like a judabuckle. She could scarcely believe what was happening. How could a ship with no engine and no controls move? Mind-patterns, she guessed, with new respect for the word.

Hundreds of meters above the ground, the bubble ship hurtled on a direct course for Smoky Top, the Mountain of the Dead. Maggie watched the panorama of moonlit obsidian, crystals, and copperdust clouds, entranced. She was so tired and her cheek throbbed so much that she had to struggle even to put two thoughts together in a sensible order. She stared through the crystal bubble in a daze. If she thought of anything at all, it was only the Mountain of the Dead, and what might be waiting there for her and Osmyrrah.

She could not say for certain just how long she spent in a half-dream, watching the ground pass far below. Quite suddenly, she rubbed her eyes, and noticed that the air in her tiny compartment had grown stuffy and moist. Breathing hard, she peered through the crystal wall at Osmyrrah, drifting safe in her water-filled bubble. When she saw Maggie looking at her, she raised her tentacle fingers in a salute.

"Os . . . Osmyrrah," Maggie gasped. "How much further? The air's running out!" She opened her mouth and panted, pressing the palms of her hands against the crystal bulkhead.

Osmyrrah seemed to be saying something, but Maggie could not make out what it was. Water and crystal transformed the words into meaningless rumbles and thumps.

"Can't . . . can't hear you," whispered Maggie. Things were starting to look foggy. She couldn't think. She felt as if she were dreaming, only she knew she wasn't. *William. Got to save William. Got to stay awake.* She repeated it to herself like the words of a magic spell. But no number of magic words kept her from sliding to the curved floor of the water lock, slipping down like a drop of water in a soap bubble.

She stretched her mouth wide and fought for air, forced her eyes to stay open, refused to let the black-winged creatures of unconsciousness descend.

Something moved in one of her pockets.

"Huh?" she groaned, almost laughing. At a time like this. Something alive in her pocket, some ugly bug or perhaps a very surprised stray judabuckle. She wanted to reach down, tear open the flap. But her hands felt like lumps of clay.

The sound of her own giggling reached her as if through an underwater cave as she watched what happened next. The pocket flap opened by itself, and one of the little glass balls Osmyrrah had given her jumped out and smashed itself against the chamber wall!

"Oh, come on," Maggie mumbled. "I've *got* to be dreaming."

But she was not. A shard from the shattered ball ricocheted into the back of her hand. "Ow!" she cried. Sitting up, she plucked the sliver out and sucked away the drops of blood. The blood tasted rusty, and very *real*.

All at once she realized that she was thinking more clearly. The air was much fresher. And in a rush of comprehension, she remembered what the glass balls were for. *If the air becomes foul, break one of these*, Osmyrrah had said.

Maggie looked up. There was Osmyrrah, her tentacles pressed against the clear wall as if she wished she could burst through it. Maggie gave her another thumbs-up. Blinking with astonishment, she reached into her pocket, brought out the other two glass balls, and stared at them. They were just featureless bubbles—no machinery, no power packs, nothing inside except highly compressed air. How could one of them have leaped from her pocket? Mindpatterns again, she thought. A fresh spark of fear raced through her at the thought of a human army trying to battle such a weapon with mere laser guns.

But she had no time to ponder the matter further, for they had reached their destination. Directly below them lay the boiling caldera of Smoky Top. They descended so quickly that Maggie felt as if her stomach would leap out of her mouth. She did not even have time to grow apprehensive about the inferno into which Osmyrrah dropped them. The bubble ship came to rest on the shore of a glowing lake of molten rock. The water lock opened, and Maggie tumbled out of the ship like a stunned skyfish from a net.

She tried to get to her feet but couldn't. Starnight seemed heavier than it should have. The mudbaby bite was a trail of fire that had now spread from her cheek down her shoulder to her arm. But in a moment, Osmyrrah stood beside her, gently helping her up, bathing her in sweet, musty fragrances that said, "Everything will be all right."

The air was so hot that Maggie found herself gasping. Within moments, perspiration soaked her coveralls and made them cling to her skin. The heavy odors of hot gases rose into the green-black sky far above like huge, invisible birds. She put up a sweaty hand to shield her eyes from the heat and glare.

"Osmyrrah!" she shouted above the boiling roar. "Where are William and Captain Stone? We've got to hurry. I can't stand this heat very long."

"Do you see the city?" said Osmyrrah. "There." And she pointed with her foremost leg.

Not far down the baked shore, Maggie made out a cluster of ruined, glittering towers. They danced and flickered in the heat waves that rose from the lava.

"Here? On the shore of a lava lake? They built a city in a horrible place like this?" she cried.

"Once it was a valley with a river. My people caused this lake. With mindpatterns."

Maggie's heart did a sudden flip-flop in her chest. "Mindpatterns did this?" They were stronger than she had ever imagined.

"Yes," said Osmyrrah, lifting Maggie onto her broad carapace. "This and many more terrible things.'' Without further explanation, she scuttled off down the rocky shore toward the ruined city.

As they approached the first of the broken crystal towers, Maggie noticed smooth, rounded objects covering the ground around its base. The brownish half-bubble shapes lay in neat circular rows like multiple strings of beads.

"What are those?" asked Maggie.

But Osmyrrah would not reply. "We must not speak," was all she would say.

When they had advanced several meters further, Maggie gasped and shut her eyes as she recognized the shapes at last. They were not smooth, brown rocks, as she had first thought. They were the dry carapaces of thousands of dead spider beasts laid side-by-side in the open air. Each carapace bore a cracked hole in the same place near its mandibles. She thought of the Smoky Top report: *each carapace smashed with some heavy, blunt object.*

Maggie swallowed hard and wiped the sweat from her forehead. She suddenly felt quite alone in a very strange land. All at once, Osmyrrah seemed just as terrifying and alien as she had on that first day in the copperdust storm. Maggie found herself longing for the simple, familiar life she had led aboard the starship Genesis, where there were no mudbabies, no spider creatures, no red-hot lakes. She yearned for cold, clean steel; the hard light of stars in the black of space; the low hum of nuclear turbines that had sung her and William to sleep. Sometimes she wondered if she belonged on a planet at all. She gritted her teeth and tried to chase these panicky thoughts from her mind. If only she weren't so tired. If only the air were cooler and the mudbaby hadn't bitten her. If only Ludlow Brak had never been born.

Maggie kept a grim silence as Osmyrrah wended her way through the field of corpses. She felt very glad for Starnight's reassuring weight and kept one hand wrapped around its bright hilt. An eternity passed before Osmyrrah scurried through a crystal doorway and down a sloping ramp of smooth stone. At the bottom of the ramp, she jolted to a stop; and Maggie, breathing hard, climbed down onto a floor of milky quartz.

"Osmyrrah," said Maggie. "Before we go any further, I'm going to ask you a question. The answer means a lot to me."

"What, Maggie?" buzzed Osmyrrah.

"Why are all those bodies smashed? Why the cracks in their carapaces?"

Osmyrrah smelled like smoke as she replied, "To release the mindpatterns. After death comes, we release the mindpatterns with the sacred crystal rod."

"But only after they're dead?" said Maggie. She held her breath. More than anything else, she wanted the right answer.

"Only then," said Osmyrrah, and Maggie breathed again. "It is an old way. We have always released the mindpatterns with the crystal. But why are you concerned?"

"I'm not. It's just something Brak said. He was trying to prove you were murderers, that's all," replied Maggie, smiling, stroking Osmyrrah's fur. "Come on. Let's find William."

The two travelers stood inside a huge crystal edifice.

Thick, glassy walls deadened the noise of the caldera outside, and the air temperature felt several degrees cooler. In the faint, warm breeze, Osmyrrah produced a rainbow of scents for which Maggie had no names. There was a watery smell that made her think of sunlight on a warm river, another smell like the sweet soil of a reed forest, and yet another fragrance like dew on the fields at dusk. They were happy smells—smells of joy. For by the light of moons and stars, and the ghostly red glow of incandescent lava that seeped through the clear walls, they could see William and Captain Stone. Their wrists and ankles were tied with ropes, but they were sitting upright on the floor not far away.

"William! Captain Stone!" Maggie cried, flooded with triumph and relief. "Is it really you?"

She could not see William's face, but she heard his urgent whisper in the darkness. "Quiet, Maggie. They'll hear you. Don't talk, just cut us free. Hurry."

Fear overwhelmed Maggie's sense of triumph as Osmyrrah silently helped her across the floor. Maggie pulled Starnight from its sheath. By its pulsing orange light, she saw Captain Stone's face crinkle into a huge smile as he whispered, "Good job, Maggie! It's wonderful to see you."

William's features looked gaunt and tight as he twisted around so that Maggie could reach his wrist ropes. "Are you okay?" she asked him as she laid Starnight's blade against the thick cord.

Almost as if in answer, a beam of bright red light cut through the darkness with a tiny buzzing sound. Maggie heard a hollow noise beside her like someone dropping a shell onto a rock. Osmyrrah fell to the ground, her legs curled up beneath her, invisible under the singed half-bubble of her carapace. She lay as still as the dead spider beasts that reposed beyond the wall, side-by-side in the open air.

"Osmyrrah!" Maggie cried in disbelief.

"Turn around slowly, my dear. Drop the sword." The voice behind her was that of Ludlow Brak.

CHAPTER TWELVE

Death by Fire

MAGGIE TURNED AROUND. SOMEONE SHONE a pocket torch in her eyes, but she could still make out three shadowy figures beyond it—one short and bald, one quite round, and one tall and wiry. Adrenaline surged through her protesting muscles once more, but she was so tired and so sick from the mudbaby venom that adrenaline no longer helped. Instead of giving her strength, it just made her shake. It made her palms wet and slippery, made a fine mist of sweat pop out on her face. It made her feel beaten, and she wanted to cry.

"You killed her!" Maggie's voice rushed out in a long, thin wail. "You killed Osmyrrah!"

Brak answered with mean laughter. "It looks that way, doesn't it? Now do as I say. Drop the sword."

For the first time in her life, Maggie felt too empty to fight. She watched her hands as if they were not really hers. They let go of Starnight; it clattered to the hard quartz floor and lay there in an undulating pool of its own light. The dancing pictures on its blade, the images of creatures and places she had never seen before, seemed to mock her. She had done her best, but her best was not good enough.

"It won't work, Brak." William's voice cut unexpectedly through the darkness. "I know what you want. You want that sword because you think it'll give you power. You think you can use it to call the Watchers, and make them do whatever you want them to, like genies from a bottle. Well, the Watchers aren't genies. And Starnight's no ordinary piece of metal. You can make Maggie drop it all right, but you'll never be able to pick it up again. There's a spell on it. Nobody can touch it but Maggie and me. Even if you could touch it, nobody can call the Watchers but me, and you'll never make me do it. Never."

"William's right, Luddy," Captain Stone said evenly. "You won't even be able to touch the sword. I know. I tried it myself once, long ago."

In reply, Brak snorted, stooped, and reached toward Starnight. He reached and reached, but he couldn't touch the sword. It lay where Maggie had dropped it. Brak's hands stopped eight or ten centimeters from the angrily pulsing blade, no matter where he tried to grasp it. Maggie watched him as if from a great distance, her arms limp at her sides. She felt like a wind-up machine that has almost run down. Osmyrrah lay still on the floor, though Maggie silently begged her to show some sign of life. Everything else seemed unimportant.

At last Brak stood up, panting and sweating. The veins in his neck and temples rose like furious worms under his skin. "What kind of game do you think

you're playing here?'' he shouted. ''People's lives are
at stake! People are going to *die* if you don't give me
the sword.''

''You don't know how wrong you are,'' cried William, straining against his ropes. ''You don't know
anything about the aliens. You think you can just walk
right in and take their city away from them without a
fight. Well, you can't. I'm telling you the truth. If you
try to attack them, we'll all die. With or without the
Watchers!''

Brak's face twisted crazily as he snarled at William
and reached once more for Starnight. Sweat gleamed
on his cheeks as he stood up empty-handed yet again.
''Fine. If this is how you want it, I can match you.
Move for move. If the sword can't be mine, then I'll fix
it so it can't be anybody's. Pick it up, Maggie.''

''Huh?'' said Maggie. Her head felt full of cotton
and her ears were ringing.

''But, Ludlow . . . '' said Zerski, lightly touching
Brak's sleeve. ''We *need* the sword. What are you
planning to . . . ''

Brak jerked away from Zerski, clenching his fists in
fury. ''Don't tell me what to do, you fool! You're no
better than the rest of these idiots.'' He turned back toward Maggie. ''I said, pick it up. We're going on a
little walk.''

''You'll be sorry for this, Brak!'' William cried, his
voice high and tight with desperation.

In a daze, Maggie knelt and picked up the sword.

''Stand up, you little fool,'' said Brak.

Maggie tried to rise. She could not make her eyes
focus. She could not stand up anymore. She didn't care.

Nothing seemed to matter much. She wanted only to lie down. Osmyrrah was dead, and she herself felt a certain coldness growing in her toes and fingers. Perhaps it was best to simply stop fighting.

Someone grabbed her by the arm and pulled her up.

"Maggie . . . Maggie, what's wrong?" William sounded far away, as if he were under water.

"Mudbaby. Poison," she heard herself mumble. She wondered if he understood.

She saw the flash of a silver tooth as Bilcher picked her up in his arms. She held fast to Starnight, afraid of losing its warmth and light, in a world that seemed to be growing steadily darker.

"I'm right behind you, Luddy," said Bilcher.

"You come, too, Zerski. We may need your help," said Brak.

Maggie watched the crystal ceiling and the ancient bubble ships that hung from it as Bilcher carried her away. The ceiling changed to green-black sky. The stars seemed very dim. She closed her eyes and there was Osmyrrah, dipping and swaying, touching her breast plate to the sand. "I am honored by you, nestling," said Osmyrrah. Maggie remembered the smells of vanilla and flour and clouds, the trace of roses and rain. She wondered if there was something she should be doing to release Osmyrrah's mindpatterns. She thought of the cracked carapaces of the spider beasts. Two tears crept down her cheeks, warm against cold. She shivered as salt water ran into the mudbaby bite. If only she were stronger. If only she could fight what was happening. If only Osmyrrah were at her side.

Someone slapped her hard on the side of her face.

"Come out of it, you little idiot. Did you hear what I said?"

There was Brak, meaty fists jammed into meaty hips, snarling like a mad cindercat. Bilcher had his hands under her arms, holding her up on her feet. The air stank of sulfur and melted rock. The roar of fire filled her ears, and curtains of heat rose in shimmering waves. She inhaled sharply as she looked down. She was standing on a black rock precipice, high above the lava lake. Her knuckles were white around Starnight's smooth, warm hilt.

"Throw the sword over!" Brak shouted in her ear, each word a distinct explosion of noise.

He wanted her to throw Starnight into the lava lake!

From some deep recess, the strength Maggie had been waiting for, though she knew it was her last, bubbled up in her heart.

"No!" she cried. "You can't make me do that!"

"I'm warning you! Do it or else!"

Maggie felt her face tighten like a steel spring wound up almost to its breaking point. She spat. Foamy saliva dribbled down Brak's cheek just below his eye.

"Throw her in!" he shrieked, his eyes green and crazy, as if no one were home behind them. "Bilcher!"

"I can't, Luddy! She's just a little girl! Are you out of your mind?"

"Throw her in!" Brak bellowed.

"Ludlow . . . Ludlow, are you sure you really want to . . ." stammered Zerski.

"What's the matter with you spineless, whining idiots? I'll do it myself, then!"

With a powerful tug, he wrenched Maggie from Bilcher's grasp. Maggie considered her situation, detached, as if she had all the time in the world. Her body was a mass of pain—ice in her arms and legs, fire in her head. There are many ways to die, she told herself. I won't go without a fight, for Osmyrrah! Nestling.

She screamed, to fend off the black shadows of unconsciousness that seemed to lurk all around her.

With that last bit of strength, Maggie pulled away from Brak and whirled like the spoked wheel of a starship. The bright sword felt like a part of her. Before she realized quite what she was doing, she caught Brak on its tip. She knew she was crying; she hated the joy she felt as she watched his face in the red lava light. Gaping mouth, wide incredulous eyes. She tried to say, "You killed her." But the words gushed out in a meaningless shriek. She pushed. And suddenly Brak was gone, over the cliff, into a death of fire.

Maggie lowered the sword, slowly, carefully. Through a haze of tears, she saw Zerski and Bilcher, huddled next to each other like frightened sheep. She wanted to say she was sorry, but her tongue wouldn't work. A tremor ran from the base of her spine upward and downward until her whole body shook and her legs gave way. She pitched to the ground. Sharp rocks cut into her knees, but she hardly felt them. Finally she understood about William—about what it meant to kill, what it meant to lose a friend, what it meant to be seen as a hero. Already, she could think of a hundred more heroic things she had done in her life.

"Don't go to sleep, Maggie. Don't go to sleep," said a voice in her ear.

"Huh . . ." she mumbled. Was she dreaming? Was it Captain Stone's voice she had heard? She could swear that she smelled . . . but it couldn't be.

A click, a buzz, and then the most wonderful sound in the universe. "Maggie. Maggie." The voice of Osmyrrah slashed through the roar of the caldera, and the fragrance of flowers and water enveloped her like a soft blanket.

"But . . . you're dead."

"No, Maggie. Not dead. The lightpistol hit only my carapace."

"But . . ."

"She's right, Maggie." William knelt beside her, his hands cool on her cheeks. She could see the red welts around his wrists where the ropes had been. She could see black burn marks in Osmyrrah's fur. "She was using one of Brak's own techniques against him. She was bluffing. Hoping for a chance to surprise him. And it worked. He left us unguarded, and she freed us. She's *alive*, Maggie. You're not dreaming. You've got to believe it."

"But I killed Brak," she said.

There was only silence for a long moment. She wondered if William had understood her.

"It's . . . it's true," Bilcher stammered.

"Yes. She pushed him over," said Zerski, motioning toward the bubbling lake.

"But he tried to push her first. She only did it to save herself," said Bilcher.

"I killed him," she whispered.

"Maggie, you did what you had to do. You didn't have a choice," said William, very close to her ear. "I know how you feel. Believe me, I know. But just stay alive, and everything will be okay. I promise you.''

Maggie sobbed weakly. ''Oh, William. I'm *so* stupid. I thought all I wanted in the whole world was to be a hero, just like you. But now I only wish none of this had ever happened.''

William shook his head. ''Take it easy, Maggie. It wasn't your fault.''

Captain Stone's commanding voice cut across the noise of the caldera. ''For the love of heaven, Zerski, Bilcher! Don't just stand there. Where's your transportation? How did you get here? We've got to get this child to the infirmary. Now!''

''They have only ground transports,'' buzzed Osmyrrah. ''I saw them. Too slow. I could take her in my bubble ship. But it is hard for her. There is too little air.'' She smelled like lightning and ammonia, so sharp it almost hurt. Maggie strained to catch some trace of rich spice. But there was none. Only the smell of fear— strong, pure, and terrible.

''If the ship is faster, we have to risk it. She's dying,'' said the captain.

Maggie felt fresh tears on her cheeks. She blinked and wished for her mother's strong, protective arms. She was afraid of the coldness that crept ever nearer to her heart. She felt Osmyrrah's soft tentacles brushing away the tears.

''All is well, nestling,'' the spider beast buzzed.

''You don't think so,'' she murmured.

''I do think so,'' said Osmyrrah.

Maggie smiled, though it wasn't easy. ''No,'' she said. ''Your smells don't match your words.''

For answer, Osmyrrah sent a wave of pungent spice, almost fierce in its intensity.

"There's another way," said William, his voice thin. "Better than ground sleds. Better than bubble ships. The Watchers." He reached for Starnight.

Maggie kept her hand wrapped around its hilt. "Are you sure, William? You don't have to. Osmyrrah could take me."

He smiled at her. "Maggie, you're as crazy as a two-star solar system. Give me Starnight, and don't worry."

The relief that flooded her when she let go of the sword was like a bath in a cool stream.

Osmyrrah used her tentacles as a pillow, so that Maggie could see what was happening. William stood apart from the others, holding the sword before him, his body bathed in its pulsing light.

"Captain, can you tell me where the constellation Orion is? Rigel, Betelgeuse, Bellatrix, any of those stars," William called, his voice clear and firm.

Captain Stone took a compass from his pocket. Droplets of sweat ran down his gray temples as he replied, "North-northwest. *That* direction, and seventy degrees from the horizon."

William closed his eyes, turned, and raised the magical sword toward the stars.

As if in a dream, Maggie watched a thin beam of red light leap from Starnight's tip and shoot out into the cold sky above. A second later, a wave of deep, hearty laughter rolled down off the crater walls and resounded across the lava lake. Maggie sobbed and smiled both at once, for she recognized that laughter. Out of the green-black night dropped something that looked like a golden star. Nearer and nearer it came, until at last it hovered above the precipice, close enough to reveal its true shape—that of a gigantic man.

"Orion!" cried William.

Maggie blinked away her tears and thought of the time she had seen the golden man through the clear dome of the starship's observation cone. She remembered everything about him. Nothing had changed. He wore the same simple tunic, wide golden belt, and heavy sandals. She remembered the shining band that held back his flowing golden hair, remembered the huge bow and the quiver filled with arrows as big as spears.

Orion's feet brushed the ground, and he stood before them grinning, his thumbs hooked into his belt.

"So, little lion," he said to William, in a voice both deep and rich. "You have called on us at last. Why have you waited so long?" His eyes glowed yellow as the heart of a friendly fire.

William lowered Starnight's tip until it rested bright and gemlike against the dark stones. A pain that he could not quite hide made his face seem tight and immobile. He looked away toward the crystal ruins, and his voice shook as he said, "I was afraid. Because of what happened to Cygnus. I was afraid Brak might . . . hurt you."

Orion reached down and with a massive hand turned William's face toward his own, more gently than Maggie would have thought possible. "If any of us are to live, little lion, we must all take risks. Cygnus knew that. And you are not to blame."

Orion stood up to his full height again. "Young ones," he said, "your task has just begun. For though Maggie has freed you from a man who would have caused death and grief, others will come to take his place. You must be vigilant."

He turned toward Zerski and Bilcher, who were still huddled against each other. "As for you," he rumbled, "hear me. I have seen creatures of such evil that the mention of their names would turn your bones to ice. You live in a universe more dangerous than you can imagine. You would do well to cultivate friendships instead of wasting your time on games of greed."

"Sir," buzzed Osmyrrah amid the cascading scent of roses and rain. "Can you help us move Maggie to safety? I am afraid."

"Yes," said Captain Stone. "It's mudbaby venom . . ."

Orion held out his hands, palms downward, as if to silence the worried questions. Slowly he nodded his huge golden head. "There is need of haste. But no need of worry."

Maggie smiled up at him and closed her eyes. Waves lapped inside her, swells and troughs. It was good when a wave came, strong and full of the power that kept her alive. But the troughs frightened her. She fought them, because she knew they meant she was dying. Was it worth it if she died, she wondered? She felt Osmyrrah warm and close to her. She thought of the spires of the alien city shining in the sun, and of the green fields of Mount Jackson. Yes, it would be worth it, to have saved all that.

She opened her eyes again, but everything seemed

unreal. The walls of the crater wavered. They almost seemed to be melting. She could still see Orion, though a cloud of golden mist enshrouded him.

She thought she heard Orion's voice, though she could not be sure. "I am taking you home, Maggie. Dream now. Dream of wonders, for all will be well."

She trusted him. At last, she let herself slip away into sleep. Brak and the lava lake and the fire in her head disappeared and were replaced by dreams of spider beasts basking on the sunlit bank of a warm river.

CHAPTER THIRTEEN

Friends

TWO DAYS LATER, MAGGIE SAT IN THE
orange noon sunlight, leaning against Osmyrrah, who
rested on the grass next to her.

"Look at that," said Maggie, pointing. "William
and Captain Stone are teaching Peaches how to play
rocket ball!"

Osmyrrah produced the cucumber pungence that
meant laughter. "It will not be fair," she buzzed. "My
nestparent has too many hands."

Maggie laughed and patted Osmyrrah's carapace,
avoiding the burned streaks from Brak's lightpistol.
She gazed up and down the banks of the Jubilation,
where colonists and spider beasts were enjoying themselves. The council had declared a holiday, with an
open invitation to the spider beasts, and the spider
beasts had graciously accepted. In the water not far
away, a large alien with white stripes in its fur showed
Josh Wedekind the basics of spider beast swimming

technique. On the grassy bank, Forest held a chunk of crystal in its tentacles and spoke earnestly to Mr. Masataka and Maggie's father. Laughter, bits of conversation, and smells of every variety wafted through the air.

"I wish I could play rocket ball, too. Or at least go swimming," said Maggie.

Osmyrrah chided her with a faint whiff of something that reminded Maggie of boot polish.

"That's right, Osmyrrah," said Maggie's mother, walking up with an armload of fat, blue mintmelons. She laid the melons on the grass, produced a long, thin powerknife from one of her belt pouches, and methodically began to slice them up.

"You know what the doctor said," she continued. "No jumping around for at least a week. You're very lucky. If it weren't for Orion and your brother, you might not be here right now. You'd better not let me catch you doing anything but lying here in the sun." She handed Maggie a dripping slice of melon, then offered one to Osmyrrah, who politely refused it.

"Mom!" said Maggie between bites, "Spider beasts don't eat, you know."

Mrs. Murdock rolled her eyes and grinned. "I know. I just didn't want to be rude, hotshot. Don't worry."

William came running up, his cheeks bright with exertion. Peaches and Captain Stone were not far behind. "Oh, boy! Mintmelon!" he cried, grabbing a big slice.

"Hello, Maggie," said Captain Stone, reaching down to tousle her hair. "Feeling more like your old self? Not so worried about . . ." he hesitated, "everything?"

For a moment, Maggie had almost forgotten about Brak, and about the cold emptiness that still crept over her every time she thought of what she had done to him. She forced herself to remember happier things— how Orion had talked to the council, how Josh Wedekind had apologized to her and William when he saw how Brak had lied. She swallowed and tried to smile at the captain. "I'm better," she said. "But I still can't forget."

Captain Stone fixed her with his kind gray eyes. "Everyone knows there was nothing else you could have done. You stopped a war, almost single-handed. Without your bravery and heroism, none of us would be here now." He patted her on the shoulder. "Can I help you slice those melons?" he called to Mrs. Murdock.

William sat down beside Maggie, wiping melon juice from his hands on the grass. "He's right, you know," he said. "Brak didn't leave you any choice."

"There's always a choice," said Maggie. "I could have thrown Starnight into the lava. Maybe Brak could have changed. Maybe we would have stopped the war anyway."

"No," buzzed Osmyrrah. "Some can never be happy, because they do not understand happiness. Brak chose his own way. He knew you would fight."

"I don't know," said Maggie. "I just wish it all could have been different."

"You did the best you could. That's all anybody can do," William said softly.

Osmyrrah added a wordless message of sweet, musty spice.

Maggie gazed across the river through half-closed eyes. It made her tired just to think about all that had happened. Or maybe it was the lingering effects of the mudbaby's venom, which had left her weak and aching. The warm sunlight poured down on her shoulders, and drowsiness touched her with inviting fingers.

Someone cleared his throat loudly. "Uh . . . we've got something for you." The voice was soft and pleasant, but it made Maggie jerk awake at once. It was also familiar, and terrible.

Bilcher stood looking down at her, his silver tooth gleaming.

"Oh, Bilcher, you're such a clod. Maggie, my dear, we've brought you a gift," said Zerski, standing beside him, beaming.

The smell of lightning escaped from Osmyrrah.

William jumped to his feet. "What's this all about?" he demanded.

Bilcher looked at his hands, tight around the handle of a wire cage. A small, purple animal scurried back and forth across its mesh floor. "Brought her a present, blast it. Wanted to say I'm . . . I'm . . ."

"He wants to say he's sorry. Honestly, Bilcher," snapped Zerski.

Bilcher scowled at him. "Well, I'm not the only one. You *said* you wanted to apologize, too!"

"All right, all right. No need to bite my head off."

"Here," said Bilcher, holding out the cage stiff-armed. "Zerski caught it. But I helped."

He looked so comical that Maggie had to squeeze her eyes shut and bite her tongue to keep from laughing. She could not manage to suppress a little smile.

"Thank you," she said as she took the cage from Bilcher. "He's a beauty! I've never seen a judabuckle so fat and shiny before. Where did you find him?"

"North of the bridge," said Bilcher.

"South of the bridge," said Zerski at the same time. They scowled at each other.

"Doesn't matter," said Bilcher. "We heard you liked judabuckles, that's all." He hesitated and looked at his feet.

"About Brak," he said, his voice low. "We're sorry. We didn't know what he was really like. I don't mind a little trickery now and then if it gets me something. But not if it's really going to hurt anybody. Brak was no good. He said we'd be important once he was in charge of things. But I don't know. He didn't care about anybody but himself."

"Yes," said Zerski, smiling pleasantly, rubbing his hands together. "Good riddance, I say."

Maggie took a very deep breath and let it out slowly, trying to conquer her horror at Zerski's reaction to his friend's death.

Captain Stone, who had been listening intently, stepped between Zerski and Bilcher, placing a firm hand on each man's shoulder. "Maggie's tired. Maybe you should be going."

Zerski sneered at the captain, grinned at Maggie, turned on his heel, and walked away. Bilcher waved as he followed. "Hope you like the judabuckle," he called.

Maggie gazed after them silently.

"They are sad," buzzed Osmyrrah. "They should live alone on the rocks in the sun until they become glad again.'' She finished her sentence with a whisper of scent like warm, dry stones that have lain untouched for a long time.

"Yes,'' said William. "They *are* sad. They're also dangerous. I think we should watch out for them, like Orion said.''

In its cage, the judabuckle dashed back and forth, squeaking.

"Poor thing,'' said Maggie. She twisted the catch and the wire door fell open. "I don't think I want any more pet judabuckles.'' The little creature flung itself out and tore through the grass to a tall stand of river reeds, where it disappeared from sight.

As Maggie watched it go, a single, vivid thought struck her. She felt much wiser and happier about the simple act of setting a judabuckle free than she did about what had happened at Smoky Top.

She laughed softly. "You know what? Being a heroine feels a lot different than I imagined.''

William nodded, as if he had guessed exactly what she was thinking. "The glory's not worth much,'' he said. "It's knowing you've done the best you can that matters.''

Both children smiled as Osmyrrah added her own comment—the happy smells of sunlight on a warm river, the sweet soil of a reed forest, and dew on a meadow at dusk.